D0381150

# The Christmas Club

## BARBARA HINSKE

Also by BARBARA HINSKE:

*Coming to Rosemont* , the first novel in the Rosemont series
*Weaving the Strands*, the second novel in the Rosemont series
*Uncovering Secrets*, the third novel in the Rosemont series
*Drawing Close*, the fourth novel in the Rosemont series
**The Night Train**
Available at Amazon and for Kindle

**I'd love to hear from you! Connect with me online:**
Visit **www.barbarahinske.com** and sign up
for my **newsletter** to receive your Free Gift, plus Inside Scoops,
Amazing Offers, Bedtime Stories & Inspirations from Home.
**Facebook.com/BHinske**
**Twitter.com/BarbaraHinske**
Search for **Barbara Hinske on YouTube** for tours inside my own
historic home plus tips and tricks for busy women!
Find photos of fictional Rosemont, Westbury, and things related to
the Rosemont series at **Pinterest.com/BarbaraHinske**.
**bhinske@gmail.com**

Library of Congress Control Number: 2016955599
ISBN: 978-0-9962747-3-9

Casa del Northern Publishing
Phoenix, Arizona

# Dedication

To my wonderful mother, Harriett Hinske, and grandmother
Pauline Stahler for making Christmas magical.

# Chapter 1

The heavy revolving door picked up speed, knocking Verna Lind's gloves out of her hand and flinging her from the warmth of the Cleveland bank into the frigid December air. Despite the flat soles of her sensible work shoes, her left foot slipped on the icy pavement, and both she and her large purse came crashing down. The purse's well-worn metal clasp burst open, spilling her possessions across the walk and into West Third Street. Dazed, Verna blinked and began to crawl toward the smattering of five-dollar bills lying in the road when a sudden gust of wind lifted her Christmas savings and sent it soaring into traffic.

Edward Fuller bent his lanky frame into the wind as he dashed down West Third Street, one hand gripping the tan fedora on his head, the other carrying a heavy briefcase. His oral argument before the court had gone well. If he hurried, he'd have time to get something to eat before his next client appointment at two thirty. He hated missing lunch. Being a bachelor, that was his only decent meal of the day.

Edward skirted the mob of people flooding from the bank's revolving door, which was in constant motion this time of year. He was almost past the exit when he saw an elderly woman burst through the door, arms flailing wildly before she tumbled to her knees. A man followed on her heels, stepped over her without offering assistance, and hurried off.

Edward pushed through the crowd to reach the woman sprawled on the ground. "Ma'am," he said, setting his briefcase on the sidewalk and squatting down next to her as she tried to get up. "Are you all right?"

Verna nodded. "I've got to get my money." She turned to him as her eyes filled with tears. "That's my Christmas money. I've saved all year. I've got to get it back."

Edward adjusted his heavy black glasses and stared. *Surely she knew that her money was gone?*

"If you haven't hurt yourself, let's help you get inside the bank," came a woman's voice over his shoulder. An easy-on-the-eyes brunette dressed in a bright red coat with fur collar and cuffs leaned over him and looked anxiously at the woman.

Verna shook her head. "I've got to get it …"

"We'll help you inside, then we'll come back outside to look for your money," the young woman insisted, placing an arm under Verna's elbow and motioning for Edward to do the same. Together, they helped Verna to her feet and escorted her back through the revolving door. They crossed the bank's lobby to a group of straight backed chairs along the wall, the young woman's high heels tapping out a staccato rhythm on the marble floor as they made their way. Verna sank into a chair without further protest.

"I'll go look for your money," Edward said. "How much did you have?'

"Thirty dollars. All in fives," Verna said. "A year's worth of savings." She shook her head. "There's no way you'll find it. It'll be long gone by now."

"You don't know that," he said. "I'm at least going to try."

"I'll find someone to bring you some water. Then I'll go help him," the young woman said, gesturing to Edward as he exited the lobby. "Will you be all right here on your own?"

Verna nodded.

"Don't leave until we come back," the young woman said before catching the eye of a banker crossing the lobby. "This woman fell in your doorway," she said. "Would you please bring her a glass of water?"

"Of course," he said, eying Verna with concern. "Should I call a doctor?"

"No, thank you. I'll just wait here until my friends return," Verna said, directing a thin smile at the young woman.

⁂

Clad in her red coat, the woman emerged from the revolving door of the bank looking like she'd stepped from the pages of a fashion magazine. Edward Fuller stood stock still, taking in the determined set of her shoulders and the graceful curves of her profile. His internal compass responded to her as if she were true north. He would later confess that was the moment. The moment that he knew—Carol Clark was "the one."

She turned her head left and then right, searching for him. He held up his hand, and she flashed *that smile*. He shook his head, and she joined him on the sidewalk.

"Nothing? What a shame," she said. "Seems like an old dear. Still working, I'd say. By the looks of her shoes, I'd guess that she's on her feet all day." She looked into Edward's eyes. "I'm heartbroken for her."

Edward nodded and pushed his glasses up on his nose. "I've had an idea, though. I've got five five-dollar bills in my wallet. I thought I'd give them to her."

"That's terribly kind of you, but I don't think she'll want your charity."

"I don't plan to tell her it's from me. I'll say we found it on the street. Tucked into the corner of a building or something. I know that will leave her five dollars short. I'd be happy to give it to her in ones, but I agree with you—I don't think she'll take it."

She smiled again and the temperature suddenly felt twenty degrees warmer to him. "I have a five in my purse," she replied. "What a nice thing for you to do. I'd be happy to contribute." She retrieved the bill from her wallet and handed it to him.

"I'm Carol Clark," she said, extending her hand once more. Edward took her hand in his own. It was warm and smooth and her handshake, firm and definite.

"Edward Fuller."

"What a lovely little Christmas secret we'll share, Edward Fuller," she said. "Let's go back in there and make that sweet lady very happy."

Verna patted the thick mass of graying blond hair secured in a bun at the nape of her neck and took a sip of her water, all the while keeping her aquamarine eyes trained on the revolving glass door. Her feet ached—as they always did after her shift at the bakery—and she was glad for the chance to sit down. She'd been sending up silent prayers that the two young people who came to her rescue would find her money—her Christmas money. It was December 15, and she'd just withdrawn all the money she'd saved in her Christmas club account.

She smiled to herself as she thought of the amount she'd been able to put aside this year. More customers were depositing their pennies and nickels in the tip jar on the counter. The attorney who came in every morning for two glazed doughnuts left a whole dollar every Friday. The economy in 1952 was booming; all the papers said so. Verna had been able to save most of her share of the tips. And she'd had thirty dollars to prove it. *Imagine that.* Eight dollars more than she'd been able to save last year. Everyone on her list would get something nice. She had next Monday off, and she'd do all of her shopping then—assuming the strangers who had stopped to help her found the bills the wind had swept away.

As the minutes ticked by, she became increasingly anxious. Asking God to help with this small request was a waste of His time. She ought to be ashamed of herself for asking Him. Verna looked at the large clock on the opposite wall. These young people were undoubtedly employed somewhere nearby and had probably already gone back to work. She'd wait another few minutes, then be on her way.

A flash of red in the revolving door caught Verna's eye before the beautiful Carol Clark stepped into the lobby. Edward Fuller was on her heels. The looks on their faces made Verna's heart race. Maybe, just maybe, her prayers had been answered. She put her hands on the arms of the chair and began to rise, but Carol motioned her to sit.

"He's found it!" she cried. "All of it! Isn't he brilliant?"

"What?" Verna gasped. "I never in a million years thought I'd see all of it again. How far did you have to look?"

"Not far, as it turns out." Edward concocted a story on the spot. "It had all gotten caught underneath a trash can across the street, where it was protected from the wind. This must be your lucky day," he said, handing her the neatly folded stack of bills.

Verna took them from his hand and opened her purse, zipping them safely into a side compartment. "I'm not taking any chances," she said, snapping the purse shut and tilting her head to smile up at them. "Thank you for taking the time to assist an old lady."

"We were glad we could help," Carol said. "You really owe it all to Mr. Fuller's quick action."

"I'm so grateful," Verna patted Edward's arm. "And now, I'd better let you two be on your way."

Edward extended his hand and helped her to her feet. "Where are you headed?" he asked.

"Home," she replied. "My bus should be along any minute."

"Let me help you to your bus stop," he said as the three of them traversed the lobby and made a slow exit out of the revolving door.

"It's just down the block, there," Verna said, pointing to a group of people waiting by the curb. She looked from one to the other. "Thank you, again, for your kindness to me. You've been my Christmas miracle. I'll put you in my prayers. And a very blessed Christmas to you both." With that, she set out for the bus stop.

Edward and Carol stood together on the pavement, watching Verna walk away. Carol turned to face him and waited.

Edward cleared his throat. "Well, Miss Clark. Very nice to meet you. Have a good afternoon."

She smiled and something flashed behind her eyes. Was it disappointment? "You too, Mr. Fuller. And a very merry Christmas."

He tipped his hat, and Carol turned and walked away. Edward checked his watch. He no longer had time for lunch and was already late for his next appointment. He set out for his office at a brisk pace, berating himself with each step. *Why hadn't he asked her out to dinner? Or at least gotten her phone number or found out where she worked?* It had been years since anyone had turned his head; he was sorely out of practice.

Edward cursed under his breath and forced his way back through the throng of people he'd just passed, retracing his steps. His long strides ate up the pavement, and his height allowed him a clear view of the other pedestrians. After three blocks he was forced to admit that he'd lost her. He slapped his thigh with his gloved hand and stomped his foot, ignoring the curious glances from passersby. *Why in the hell had he been so slow—so stupid?* If there really were Christmas miracles, maybe he would see Carol Clark again.

# Chapter 2

Art Burkowski instinctively threw out his left arm, grabbing the light post on the busy corner of West Third and Superior to steady himself. Seeing a child nearby, he suppressed the oath that sprang to his lips and looked down at his offending footwear. His right shoe was untied, again. He squatted down to tie his shoe, this time securing it with a double knot.

As he rose, a green rectangular piece of paper fluttering against the light post caught his attention. He took a closer look. A five-dollar bill, crisp and perfect, was pinned to the post by the strong winds.

Art carefully removed the bill and looked to the people heading purposefully one way or another, rushing to get into the shops and out of the icy wind. Seeing no one casting about for something lost, Art tucked the bill into his pants pocket, satisfied, and continued on his way.

He was headed to the Terminal Tower train station to buy a ticket home. For the first time since the war was over, he'd have the whole week off at Christmas. With this extra five dollars, he'd buy himself a first-class ticket and travel in high style for once in his life.

The ticket window was busy, and Art took his place at the back of a long, slow-moving line. He unbuttoned his coat and loosened the heavy muffler wound around his neck, revealing a white lab coat with his name embroidered on the pocket. His grandmother had given it to him when he'd graduated from pharmacy school and she'd done the stitching herself. He ran his hand absently over the bumpy letters. His grandmother's health was failing, and Art needed to get home before it was too late. After what seemed an eternity, he moved up to the ticket window and removed his wallet from his pocket.

"Where to?" the ticket agent asked.

"Albany," Art said. "The Sunday afternoon train, please."

The man grimaced. "That's a very popular route." He consulted a ledger in front of him. "Sold out. I'm terribly sorry, sir."

Art sighed. "It doesn't really matter. Put me on the next one."

"It's not that simple, sir. With Christmas coming, everything's booked."

"I thought I was buying my ticket in plenty of time." Disappointment radiated from him. "I haven't been home for the holidays in years. My grandmother is eighty-seven, and my mother thinks this may be her last Christmas. They'll be so disappointed. Is there anything you can do?" he pleaded.

The ticket agent thumbed through a stack of train schedules on his desk. He pursed his lips and made notes on a scratch pad. "I can get you there with changes in Pittsburgh and Philadelphia." He looked up at Art. "That trip will take you much longer than the direct route. You'd start out on the late-afternoon train to Pittsburgh on Christmas Eve and get to Albany after suppertime on Christmas day."

Art released the breath he'd been holding. "That's swell. As long as I'm there on Christmas, that's all that counts."

The ticket agent smiled. "We'll get you home for Christmas. And the only seat left for the Cleveland to Pittsburgh leg is in first class, so I'll let you have that at no extra charge. Maybe that'll make up for the extra-long journey."

"That's awfully kind of you, sir. I appreciate it very much." Art handed him the fare.

The ticket agent nodded. "Glad to do it." He slid the ticket across the counter to Art. "Go have yourself a merry Christmas."

Art carefully placed the ticket into his pocket, his hand brushing the five-dollar bill he had recently found on the street. He set out for the exit.

He was halfway across the main concourse when he passed a shoe-shine man attempting to drum up business. He looked down at his worn footwear; there would be no point in engaging the man's services for his shoes.

He continued on, when a thought struck him. He turned back and a smile spread from ear to ear. He reached into his pocket and, as the shoe-shine man continued to solicit customers, Art Burkowski removed the five-dollar bill from his pocket and slipped it into the man's tip jar.

# *Chapter 3*

Edward Fuller checked his watch as he entered the main concourse of Terminal Tower. He had at least thirty minutes before his appointment at 10 a.m. on the fourteenth floor. He scanned the busy area, searching for something to occupy his time. He saw a newsstand on the opposite corner and made his way through the crowd. He'd pick up *The Plain Dealer* and relax for a few minutes.

He paid for the paper and went in search of a place to sit. He was headed for a bank of benches along the perimeter when he noticed a shoe-shine stand. Edward looked at his shoes. Although he polished them without fail every Sunday evening, they could do with some professional attention.

He waited patiently as the proprietor finished with his customer.

"Don't worry about your son, Mr. Rosen. He's a smart boy—a good boy. He's just young and doesn't want his daddy making his way for him. He wants to do for himself."

The man nodded as he the proprietor took his arm and helped him out of the elevated chair. "I suppose you're right. I always feel better after I've talked with you, Carter," he said. "You expect good things to happen, don't you?"

"Yes sir. And they always do. Merry Christmas, sir."

"And to you, too," the man said, patting Carter Williams on the back. He reached into his pocket for his money clip and dropped a tip into the jar.

"Thank you kindly," Carter Williams said as Edward took a seat.

Carter smiled at him broadly. "How we doin' today, sir? Life treating you well?"

"Fine, thanks," Edward replied.

The man wiped his rag over Edward's shoes. Edward removed his glasses, cleaned them with his handkerchief, and opened his newspaper.

Carter began to whistle, moving from one Christmas carol into the next.

Edward tossed the newspaper aside. "You're in a jubilant mood, today," he remarked.

"Every day's a good day, sir. I'm the luckiest man I know." He pointed to his rack of polishes and brushes and patted the chair that Edward was sitting in. "I own all of this. I'm my own boss. If I want a day off, I take a day off. If I want to move to Florida, I move to Florida. I make all the money I need to eat and keep a roof over my head. And sometimes—on days like today—really special things happen."

Edward couldn't help but smile. "That does sound pretty appealing. I'm booked all day long. It takes me months to schedule an afternoon off."

"See what I say?" Carter beamed.

"So what happened to you today that was so special, if I might ask?"

"I'm happy to tell you," Carter said. "My morning started out real slow. I got here at seven thirty to shine businessmen's shoes on their way to work. Nobody stopped—not one person. I even stepped into the concourse to drum up business. Nuthin'." He shrugged. "I was feeling down in the dumps. This is Christmas and I've got gifts to buy. I came in real early so's I could get some extra. I was over there," he said, pointing. "Trying to catch men coming up from the train, and I see a guy leaning over the tip jar. I figure he's trying to see if there's money in there he can take since nobody's around." He shook his head. "I'm not that stupid. I always take my tip money outta the jar when I leave. I was hurrying to get back to my stand to say something to him, but a bunch of people got in my way, and when I got around them, he was gone."

Carter paused and leaned back on his stool to look at Edward. "I went over to my tip jar, and you wouldn't believe what I found."

Edward raised an eyebrow and gestured to the man to continue.

"There was a five-dollar bill in the jar! Imagine that. A five-dollar bill. I didn't even give the guy a shoe shine."

Edward grinned. "Sounds like that man had the holiday spirit. I'm glad for you."

"Here I was feelin' sorry for myself—losing faith—when the Good Lord sends a man to give me money," Carter said. "That's more than what I would have made if I'd been busy all mornin'." He completed his work on Edward's shoes. "Goes to show—never lose faith that God will provide."

Edward paid Carter and carefully folded a five-dollar bill and slipped it into the tip jar. He wished Carter a very merry Christmas as he stepped back onto the concourse. The man's advice to "never lose faith that God will provide" was running through his mind when he saw—along the opposite side of the concourse—a young brunette in a red coat walking briskly toward the exit.

Edward resisted his instincts for a split second, then threw caution to the wind and started across the concourse at a trot. He wove through the crowd, murmuring "Excuse me" as he jostled his way across the stream of people. He lost sight of the red coat momentarily but picked it up again as she went out the exit. He picked up speed, barreling through the last forty feet, and shot through the door onto the sidewalk. Edward scanned the crowd, searching frantically for a woman in a red coat. *There was no sign of her.*

He checked his watch; he prided himself on being punctual. If he hurried, he could make it back to the elevator in time for his meeting.

But instead of turning around, Edward crossed the street. Maybe Carol Clark had slipped into one of the small shops or cafés along the block. It would only take a moment to look.

He moved along the street, stepping in and out of each establishment, looking for the red coat. *Why in the world was this so important to him?* He'd only met her once—and briefly, at that. He had enough on his plate, working long hours at his growing practice and supporting his widowed sister and her two children. The last thing he had time for was a girlfriend, as he frequently reminded his sister when she tried to fix him up with eligible women. He shook his head. *There was no denying it; there was something about this Carol Clark.*

Edward reached the roasted nut purveyor at the far end of the block. The heady aroma filled the air. He glanced through the plate-glass window of a nearby café, and his heart skipped a beat when he caught a glimpse of red at the crowded counter inside. He squeezed into the small space and craned his neck to see over the customers in front of him. His heart sank when he saw it was a substantially older woman, clad in a red peacoat.

Edward eased out of the shop and retraced his path to Terminal Tower, cursing himself under his breath for his foolishness. Now he would be late for his meeting.

<hr>

Carol Clark stepped out of the ladies' room of the café where she'd stopped to pick up a sandwich to take back to her desk. She pushed her way out the door in time to see a tall man stride past her, adjusting his glasses with one hand and gripping a briefcase with the other. She turned in the opposite direction and set off toward the law firm where she worked.

There was something familiar about that man, she mused, as she walked along the busy downtown sidewalk. Carol was halfway down the block when the realization hit her. She spun on her heel, turning to retrace her steps. The man was Edward Fuller.

She hurried her steps. *Why in the world was she racing after a man she barely knew?* Lots of men had been interested in courting her since her fiancé Ken had been killed in the Pacific. She reached the street corner as the light changed to red, forcing her to come to an abrupt halt. She had to admit—no man had caught her fancy during those nine long years alone like Edward Fuller had. She sidled to the edge of the pedestrians waiting to cross the street and stood on her tiptoes, trying to catch another glimpse of him, but there was no trace.

Carol sighed and sank back into the crowd. *He was gone.* He'd been on her mind since their chance meeting outside the bank yesterday. And now he'd been less than ten feet from her and was gone again. She put her hand to her cheek. *Why was she so smitten with Edward Fuller?*

The light changed and she felt the pedestrians around her push forward. She elbowed her way out of the crowd and resumed her lonely walk back to her office.

# Chapter 4

Rosemary Payne checked her watch, shifting her weight from her right foot to her left, cursing the stiff heels on her pumps. She was wearing a blister on her right foot. At the rate the line was moving, she'd be late getting back to the office. Her boss didn't tolerate tardiness. The layaway line wouldn't get any shorter this close to Christmas, and she had to do this during her lunch hour. Mr. Hamlin was out to lunch with that nice Mr. Fuller, so he'd probably be gone longer than an hour himself. With any luck, she'd be in her seat when they returned to the firm.

Rosemary shuffled forward as another customer paid off their account and retrieved their items. The woman in front of her stepped to the counter and took a tattered envelope out of her purse, removing two crumpled dollar bills and a handful of change.

The woman leaned over the counter as the cashier counted the money and made an entry in a ledger. The cashier looked up and shook her head. The woman's shoulder's sagged.

Rosemary leaned forward.

"What can I get?" she heard the woman ask.

"You can take two of the toys," the cashier replied. "And this close to Christmas, if you don't take the third, we'll put it back out on the floor."

"But I have three children," the woman protested. "I can't leave one out."

The cashier straightened and looked at the woman. "I can't make an exception for you. That'd get me fired. You can take two of the toys or you can come back when you've got the rest of the money. Remember, you've got to pay this off before Christmas Eve."

The woman nodded slowly. "What time do you close on Christmas Eve?"

"Two o'clock. We close the layaway line at noon."

"I'll be back," the woman said. "I'll find the money."

The cashier pointed to Rosemary. "Next, please."

The woman stepped aside, and Rosemary moved to the counter. "Sorry to take so long," the woman murmured as they passed each other.

Rosemary looked into the woman's eyes. She gave Rosemary an embarrassed smile. Rosemary swallowed hard. She didn't have children of her own, yet, but could imagine how this woman felt. She'd had to put toys for her nephews on layaway, but she had enough to pay them off today. When she boarded the train for Pittsburgh on Christmas Eve, she'd have a suitcase full of nice gifts for her family. She even had five dollars extra after she'd found that bill on the street earlier in the week. She'd been thinking of what she'd spend it on—now she knew.

The cashier cleared her throat, one hand resting on the open ledger book. "Account number, please."

"Wait," Rosemary said. "Before you lose your place—I'd like to pay five dollars towards that woman's account."

The cashier stared at Rosemary.

"Will five dollars help her?"

The cashier nodded. "Yes—it'll more than pay off her account. In fact, she'd have a small credit."

Rosemary smiled. "Good. That's fine." She removed the five-dollar bill that she'd folded and placed into her wallet. "When she comes in, will you tell her it's from Santa?"

"I most certainly will." The cashier patted Rosemary's hand. "That's very nice of you, dear."

"I couldn't help but overhear. She was in a horrible predicament."

"I see some heartbreaking things, working back here in layaway. Especially this time of year. People put money on things for months and then they lose a job or somebody gets sick, and they can't pay. That woman you're helping," she said, leaning close to Rosemary. "She's been coming in every week since July. Her husband's a carpenter but he got hurt on the job and doesn't work much. She's always scraping together her pennies and dimes to bring in here."

"I found that five on the street this week. It was odd that I found it at all. I was in the middle of a group of people, waiting for the light to turn so we could cross the street. I looked down at my shoes and there it was. Any one of us could have seen it."

The cashier raised an eyebrow.

"It was like God wanted me to have that money. I've been wondering all week if there was something I was meant to do with it."

"Most people would have spent it on themselves without a second thought." The cashier completed the notation she was making in the ledger. "I can't wait to see her face when I tell her Santa paid off her layaway. That'll be fun for me, too."

The two women smiled at each other. "I like the thought of that," Rosemary said.

"Now," the cashier said, folding her hands over the ledger, "did you have money for your account?"

"Yes." She pulled the necessary amount from her wallet. "I think this will pay it off."

Rosemary hung her coat in the cloakroom off of the lobby and hurried down the corridor to her desk. She glanced into her boss's office and was dismayed to see that Mr. Hamlin had, indeed, beat her back from lunch. He was hunched over a stack of documents on his desk, red pencil in hand. She slipped into her chair and placed her purse on the floor at her feet.

"Ahhh … there you are." Mr. Hamlin stood in the door to his office, fidgeting with his red pencil. "Can you come in here, please?"

Rosemary swallowed. She'd labored all morning, typing the seventh revision of the complicated estate plan he was currently working on. Mr. Hamlin didn't tolerate any mistakes on his papers; she must have overlooked a flaw in her proofreading. Rosemary steeled herself for his rebuke as she followed him into his office.

"Sit down, won't you?" He gestured to the chair on the other side of his desk.

She lowered herself slowly into the seat and folded her hands in her lap. She'd never been invited to sit before.

Howard Hamlin cleared his throat. "How long have you been with me, Rosemary?"

"Three and a half years, sir."

Hamlin nodded. "I don't think I've told you that you're doing a terrific job."

Rosemary stared at him.

"I've been practicing law a long time, and you're the best secretary I've ever had. I know I'm not the easiest person to work for; I'm precise and demanding." He glanced at Rosemary.

"People's estates are important to them. They have a right to expect them to be perfect. I know that you care about your clients and take pride in your work. I've always done my best, but sometimes I make mistakes." Her gaze traveled to the papers on his desk, now covered in red marks.

"These? I've made revisions—they're not your errors." He looked back at her. "I didn't call you in here to reprimand you about these." His hand brushed over the documents on his desk. "I've been reminded of several things recently—very recently."

As recently as lunch with that nice Mr. Fuller, Rosemary suspected.

"I don't praise you enough—and I don't pay you enough." He coughed and reached into his desk drawer and handed Rosemary a piece of paper.

Her brows shot up as she unfolded the paper and a check slipped to her lap.

"I'd like you to have that, as a Christmas bonus. I've written your new salary, beginning in January, on the paper."

Rosemary gasped. "This is very generous, sir." She clutched the paper and the check to her chest. "Thank you."

"You're most welcome, Rosemary. You've earned it."

Rosemary got to her feet. "I can stay late tonight, retyping those papers, if you need me to," she said, pointing to his desk.

"We'll take these up tomorrow. In fact, why don't you take the rest of the afternoon off to finish your Christmas shopping?"

Rosemary had to make a concerted effort to prevent her mouth from dropping open. She hurried to her desk and picked up her purse. She didn't know what Edward Fuller had said to her boss, but she was grateful. She'd received a bonus, a raise, and the afternoon off instead of a reprimand. This was her own Christmas miracle.

# Chapter 5

Larisa Denisovich clutched the hand of her grandson as they inspected the trees in the Christmas tree lot four blocks from their apartment building. Six-year-old Sasha was mesmerized by the row of towering Douglas fir, Scotch pine, and Colorado blue spruce. Larisa gently pulled his hand, steering him to the back of the lot toward the smaller trees.

"We have to carry the tree up the stairs. We need to get something we can manage." She didn't add that they had to find a tree she could afford.

Sasha reluctantly trailed his grandmother.

Larisa smiled down at him. "We'll decorate it with strings of popcorn and cranberries and those ornaments I made with fabric remnants from the shop. By the time we're done, it'll look grand." She certainly hoped so. Sasha had come up with the idea of surprising his mother with a Christmas tree of their own this year. They'd never had one in the twenty years since she and her late husband, Peter, and their little Anna had left their home to come to America. Now that Peter was gone, she was determined to carry on with the tailoring shop and honor her deathbed promise to him to make sure Anna and Sasha were happy.

They walked down the line of trees, examining each one from every angle. They stood, pointing to a nicely shaped Douglas fir, as the proprietor approached them.

"Have you made your selection?" he asked.

Sasha nodded vigorously.

"I'll tie it to your car," the older man said, reaching through the branches to grasp the trunk.

"We don't have a car. We'll be carrying it home."

The man eyed the petite older woman and the small boy. "How far do you have to go?"

"Just four blocks down, the fourth apartment building on the right," she pointed down the street. "And up to the third floor. We live in number 315."

"I can let you borrow a wagon to take it to your building if you promise to bring it right back." He tussled Sasha's golden curls.

"Thank you. But first I need to know—how much is it?" Larisa asked.

"All of these are five dollars."

Larisa gasped. "So much?"

The man looked at her and nodded. She turned aside.

"They'll be on sale on Christmas Eve," he replied softly. "Everything will be half price on Christmas Eve. If there are any left—sales are strong this year."

Larisa nodded and sighed deeply. "We'll take our chances and come back on Christmas Eve." Business had been slow at the shop, and all she had was three dollars. She shouldn't even be spending that much, she reminded herself.

Larisa put her hand on Sasha's shoulder. "We'll get our tree later," she told him. His solemn expression told her he understood why they were leaving without their Christmas tree. She swallowed the lump in her throat and led Sasha toward the exit.

They passed a tall man in a heavy overcoat as they moved through the opening in the chain-link fence that surrounded the lot. The man doffed his hat, revealing a head of bright red hair, neatly combed to the side.

"Hello, Mr. Park," she said. The man was one of her regular customers.

"Picking out your tree?" he asked. "My wife told me I'd better come home with ours today, or we might not get one." He gestured to the half-empty Christmas tree lot. "She said they're selling fast."

"I think we're going to look around a bit more."

"Ahhh … well. Don't leave it too long or you'll go without." He grinned at Sasha. "We wouldn't want this little guy to wake up on Christmas morning without a tree."

Larisa tugged on Sasha's hand and moved away swiftly. "Merry Christmas, Mr. Park," she said over her shoulder.

"And to you," Tony Park called after her. He replaced his hat on his head and sought out the proprietor. "Show me your tallest trees," he told the man. "I'm not going to shop around, like that lady and little boy that just left." He gestured to the entrance with his head. "I'm here to buy."

The proprietor led him to a twelve-foot blue spruce. "I don't think they were shopping around. They couldn't afford a tree."

Tony halted and looked at the older man. "Are you sure?"

"Positive. They'll come back on Christmas Eve, but at the rate we're selling trees, we'll be cleaned out and closed up by this weekend. We're not getting another shipment."

Tony rocked back on his heels and released a deep breath. "I'm an idiot. No wonder she was rather curt with me. I must have embarrassed her."

The man shrugged. "I'm sure you didn't know."

"I didn't." He shook his head. "She's such a hard worker, and she deserves a break. What a shame. Some people have all the luck. Like me—I found a five-dollar bill on the street this week. Practically blew into my hand."

The proprietor stepped closer to the tree he'd suggested.

"I'll take it," Tony said, reaching for his wallet. "And I'd like to buy one for Mrs. Denisovich and that kid. If I pay for a tree, can you save it for her?"

"I can do better than that," the man replied. "I can deliver it to her. She lives in an apartment down the street. Delivery will be on the house."

Tony smiled and clapped the man on the shoulder.

"She was looking at the five-dollar trees. I can show you the one they liked."

Tony shook his head. "I think I can do better than that. Let's pick out a nice seven-footer."

⌒⌒

The proprietor was wrestling the chain-link gate into place as a car turned into the nearby parking lot, illuminating him in its headlights. He waved and shook his head no as he

31

continued to pull the gate into place. It had been a long day. He'd been on his feet for twelve straight hours, without even a chance to eat the sandwich he'd packed for himself that morning. He still needed to put together the deposit, head to the bank's overnight drop box, and deliver the tree to that woman in the apartment down the street. These last-minute shoppers would just have to come back in the morning.

Tony Park pulled his car up to the gate and cut the headlights. He leapt out and called to the proprietor, who was walking quickly back into the lot. "Have you delivered the tree to Mrs. Denisovich?"

The proprietor turned back. "I didn't realize it was you. Not yet. I'm going to take it to her after I make the bank deposit."

"If we wouldn't hold you up, could we come in and decorate it first?" Tony gestured to his car. "My wife suggested that we put lights on the tree, and my daughters thought it would be fun to decorate the whole thing. So we bought lights and ornaments, and here we are."

The proprietor approached the gate, the weariness he had felt moments before vanishing.

"We won't be long. With the four of us working together, it shouldn't take us more than thirty minutes."

The man opened the gate. "I'll go make my bank deposit. You should be done by the time I get back."

Tony turned toward the car and motioned with his hand for his family to join him. "I'll help you take it to her front door, but I don't want to be there when you ring the bell."

"That's the fun part," the proprietor said. "Don't you want to see her reaction?"

"I'll leave that for you," Tony said as his wife and daughters joined him. Each of them carried large shopping bags containing lights and decorations.

"I pulled the tree over there by the office," the proprietor said, pointing. "You get busy, and I'll finish up my deposit." He hummed as he totaled the day's take, and the Parks sprang into action.

The two men rounded the corner on the second-floor landing and took the tree up the remaining steps to the third floor. They set the tree into its stand and Tony adjusted a string of lights that had gone askew on the trip up the stairs. They were both breathing heavily.

"Thanks for helping me. This would have been miserable on my own."

Tony smiled and shrugged. "It looks pretty good, doesn't it?"

"I've never seen a prettier tree," the proprietor said. "And I've seen a lot of trees. Are you sure you don't want to give it to her yourself?"

Tony shook his head. "I've got to go. My wife and kids are waiting for me. Can you take it from here?"

"Piece of cake," the proprietor said. "Her apartment is right over there." He pointed to a door on the other side of the hallway.

"Merry Christmas," Tony said, extending his hand.

"And to you," the man replied as they shook.

Tony was halfway to the second floor when he heard the man's firm knock on Mrs. Denisovich's door. He paused to listen. He couldn't make out what the proprietor said, but heard a door creak open and then a woman's high-pitched exclamation in a language he didn't understand. Her voice was soon joined by the excited cries of a child. Tony smiled broadly and continued down the stairs, two at a time.

"What is this?" Larisa asked. "We didn't buy this tree. You've made a mistake."

"No ma'am," the older man said. "There's no mistake. This tree was a sample tree on our lot. We can't sell it with the lights and ornaments already on it. Nobody wants to buy a decorated tree." He paused and looked closely at Larisa. Her wide eyes and open smile told him she didn't question his story. He continued. "We'll sell out of trees tomorrow and close the lot. I'd have to put this tree in the dumpster. That seemed such a waste."

Larisa nodded in agreement.

"I was hoping that you hadn't found a tree somewhere else. I thought you might be able use this one."

Larisa's smile lit every corner of her face.

"You'd be doing me a favor," he added.

"We'd love to do you a favor," she said, motioning him inside.

❦

Larisa rose early the next morning and set to work quietly in the kitchen. Her daughter and grandson were still sleeping soundly in the tiny living room.

Sasha had been so excited about the Christmas tree that Anna had finally given up trying to tuck him into bed. They'd all gotten into their heavy flannel pajamas and brought their pillows and blankets into the tiny living room. They'd turned out all of the lights except for those on the Christmas tree and Anna and Sasha had fallen asleep in their glow.

Sleep had evaded Larisa and she remained awake, contemplating the kindness of the man she had met only that afternoon. She hadn't been taken in by his story; she knew he was doing them a kindness. Shortly before midnight, an idea struck her. She'd retreated to her bed, vowing to awaken early enough to make pastilas before she left for work. She would take this man a plate of the Russian delicacy that had won her grandmother acclaim in the old country.

⁘

Larisa walked gingerly on the icy sidewalk, carrying a glass plate wrapped in waxed paper and tied with a red ribbon. The outline of the colorful treats was visible through the paper. She'd collected her parcel as soon as she arrived home from work, anxious to deliver her gift before the kind man closed up shop.

She quickened her pace the last few yards and was relieved to see the gate ajar, even though the *Closed* sign was prominently displayed. Larisa squeezed through the opening into the lot. Other than the shack in the corner bearing a sign that read, "Office," and a small stack of browning trees lying on their side by a dumpster, the lot was empty.

She knocked on the door of the office but got no response. "Hello?" she called through the door. She tried the knob and found it locked. Her hand fell to her side, and she leaned her forehead against the wooden door. Now she'd never be able to thank the kind man.

Larisa turned and was making her way back to the gate when an old red pickup pulled into the lot. Relief flooded over her as the proprietor stepped from behind the wheel. She raised her hand in greeting.

"I'm so glad I caught you," she called as he approached.

"Is everything all right with your tree?" he asked.

"It's perfect. I wanted to thank you." She extended the plate of pastilas to him.

"You didn't have to do this," he protested.

"It's my pleasure. You know pastilas?"

He shook his head.

"They're Russian pastries. My grandmother made them and won many prizes. She was famous for her pastilas." Larisa smiled at him. "I made these this morning. I think you'll like. Take them home to your wife and family."

The proprietor flushed. "I'm a widower."

"Then you can enjoy them all yourself."

He nodded. "This is very kind of you. Thank you."

"I was afraid I'd missed you," she said, pointing to the empty lot.

"I just finished my last delivery. I'm going to put those trees in the dumpster and lock up. I'm done for another year."

Larisa resumed her progress to the gate.

"I'll only be a moment," he called. "If you can wait, we can go for a cup of coffee and then I can drive you home?" He smiled at her.

Larisa ran her eyes over his face. *Here is a good, kind man,* she thought. "I'd love to. Pastilas are perfect with coffee."

# Chapter 6

Edward Fuller descended the stairs two at a time, pulling up at the last minute to let Stanley beat him to the bottom. Stanley landed in the hallway and took off at a run. "Beat you!" he cried over his shoulder as he rounded the corner into the kitchen.

Edward followed at a leisurely pace. His favorite part of the week was Saturday morning, which he spent with his nephew. He grinned at his sister, who was busy pouring batter into the electric skillet he'd given her. She'd protested that she didn't need such conveniences, but he knew she enjoyed them. Nancy smiled in return and nodded toward the coffee pot. "It's fresh," she said, wiping her hands on a bright yellow dish towel bearing a map of Florida. "Pancakes will be ready in a few minutes. There's bacon, too."

"Quite the spread for a Saturday morning," he commented. "How'd we get so lucky?"

She reached for the platter, now empty, where she'd placed the bacon. "Stanley," his mother reprimanded. "That's not all for you. Your uncle and I both want some of that. Two strips for everyone. Put the rest back."

Stanley studied his plate and selected the four smallest slices of bacon to return to the platter.

"I've got to be at church early tomorrow. The choir needs extra warm-up time. We're doing some really special Christmas music. So you'll be on your own for breakfast." She flipped the pancakes over with her spatula.

"That's fine," Edward replied. "I can pour cereal into a bowl with the best of them."

"Will you bring the boys with you when you come? And why don't you stay for coffee after the service? There's a new girl in the choir that I'd like you to meet."

Edward held up both hands in a defensive gesture. "I'll bring Stanley to church—and Jim, if he wants to come—but I think I'll pass on meeting the new girl."

Nancy pursed her lips. "Why do you resist my efforts to help you meet someone? Don't you want to get married?"

"I appreciate the thought, but I'll find someone on my own." He held out their plates as she slid three pancakes onto each one.

"You don't seem to be getting anywhere on that front," she said. "I just think you could use some help. I've introduced you to a lot of fine young women who would love to be married to a nice, successful man like you."

"Like I said, I appreciate it, but I haven't had anything in common with any of them."

"That's because you're way too picky," Nancy grumbled.

"Stanley, pass the syrup to your mother. What do you want to do today?" he asked his eleven-year-old nephew.

"You need to stop at the library, first," Nancy interjected. "I've got a stack of books to go back, and Stanley needs to pick out a biography to read over

Christmas break. He has a book report due on the week he goes back to school."

"Aw, Mom," Stanley began to protest.

"Good idea," Edward interrupted him. "We'll do that first, then go to the movies. Eat popcorn until we bust." He ruffled Stanley's hair.

Stanley slid off his chair and took his empty plate to the sink.

"I'll wash the breakfast dishes," Nancy said. "Go brush your teeth and make your bed. And run a comb through that mop of yours."

Edward caught Stanley's eye and jerked his head toward the stairs. "I'm going to have an extra cup of coffee. When you've done that, we'll get started." He rose and brought the coffee pot to the table, pouring a second cup for his sister and then himself.

Nancy studied her brother over the rim of her cup, blowing on the steaming liquid. "You're very good to us, Edward. I'll always be grateful." She lowered her eyes to the table. "You've done a great job with my boys. Stanley will remember you more than he will his own father."

"It was a crime that Norman died of diphtheria. You were such a happy family." He leaned toward her and caught her eye. "Why haven't you remarried? Why are you so worried about my love life when you should be focusing about yours?"

Nancy looked long into her brother's eyes. "It'll always be Norman for me. And only Norman. I'm still as in love with him as the day we met. I don't have room in my heart for anyone else."

Edward opened his mouth to speak, but she put up a hand to stop him. "I don't think that's the smartest thing for me to do, but that's my decision. Your situation is different, Edward."

Edward shifted uncomfortably in his chair.

"I know that you loved Kathy. She was a fool to run off with that low-life salesman from Detroit instead of waiting for you to come home. I'll bet she regrets her decision."

Edward shrugged and adjusted his glasses.

"You threw yourself into law school, and you've made something of yourself." Nancy took a sip of her coffee. "I've never told you this, but I didn't like Kathy. She wasn't good enough for you, by half. I was relieved when she married somebody else. I'm just sorry that she's made you gun-shy about marriage. All women aren't like Kathy."

"I know that, Nancy. I'm not opposed to getting married. I've just been too busy to find someone new."

She patted his hand and continued. "You're a family man, Edward. Look how you dote on me and the kids." She pointed to the electric skillet. "You need to have the joy of your own wife and children. I love you very much, and I am not going to sit still and allow you to miss the greatest happiness of life. That's why I keep introducing you to eligible women. I want to see you happily married, and you don't seem to be making any progress on your own."

Nancy picked up their plates and began to rise from the table. "So will you at least let me introduce you to this girl at church?"

Edward sighed, then shrugged.

"Good," she said. "Then it's settled. I think she's someone that you could be very happy with."

Edward carried their coffee cups to the sink. He couldn't shake the feeling that he'd already met someone he could be very happy with, and her name was Carol Clark.

❦

Edward opened the door of the public library, allowing a blast of bitterly cold air to enter with them. He and Stanley stepped onto the carpeted floor mats and stamped the snow off of their boots.

"Do you know who you'd like to do your report on?"

Stanley shook his head. "It stinks that we have to read a book over Christmas."

"Reading a book isn't going to kill you. We'll find someone interesting. You'll get bored on break and will be glad you have it."

Stanley shot his uncle a skeptical look. They stepped through the second set of doors into the majestic main reading room. Edward leaned close to his nephew and swung his arm in an arc to encompass the massive marble columns and carved vaulted ceiling. "I used to love coming here as a kid," Edward said. "I always left with an armload of books. You can find the answer to almost any question in here. You can visit places and have adventures you'll never have in real life. I just wish I had time to read."

"You read all day long at your job, don't you?" Stanley asked.

"Legal briefs and court decisions. I'm talking about pleasure reading." Edward put his hand on Stanley's shoulder. "Let's go ask the lady at the desk if she can tell us where to find biographies."

Stanley reluctantly followed his uncle.

Janet Hatcher smiled at the man and boy as they approached. She removed the glasses from the end of her nose and let them rest on their chain against her ample bosom. "Good morning. How are the two of you today?"

Edward pressed Stanley forward and gestured toward the woman with his head. "Fine, ma'am," Stanley stammered.

"I'll bet you're looking for something for a book report, aren't you?"

Stanley nodded.

"Thought so. The schools send us lists of the Christmas break reading assignments so we can be ready for students when they come in."

"That's smart," Edward said.

Janet cocked her head to one side and regarded Stanley thoughtfully. "You're in fifth grade?"

Stanley smiled and relaxed his shoulders.

She checked her list. "Biography. Good—I was hoping that was it. We've got the best selection of biographies all pulled onto trolleys in the second room on the right," she said, pointing to a hallway that lead away from the reading room. "What are you interested in? Pirates? Soldiers? Ancient Rome?"

Stanley shrugged. "All of those, I guess. I thought we'd have to read about kings or presidents."

Janet Hatcher put the *Back in a Moment* sign at the front of her desk. "You're one of the first to come in to select your book. Very smart of you," she said, winking at Edward. "The best books are still available. If you came in after Christmas, the really exciting ones would be gone. Let me take you back to show you what we've got. Biography is one of our most popular categories, and I'll point out my favorites."

The librarian set off at a brisk clip that belied her age and Edward and Stanley fell in line behind her.

# Chapter 7

Carol Clark stepped into the main reading room of the library and deposited the heavy stack of books she was carrying into the book return bin. She opened her purse and removed the list of books, written in her mother's neat hand. Carol ran this errand for her mother every other week and usually enjoyed spending time in the familiar space, often picking out a book or two for herself. Today, however, she was in a hurry. She had a dance to go to tomorrow afternoon—her first dance in years—and she wanted to buy a new dress and shoes. She was nervous about going, and a new outfit would bolster her confidence. She planned to pick up her mother's books, deposit them at home, and catch a bus to Higbee's massive department store downtown to do her shopping.

Carol stepped up to the desk and noted with disappointment the *Back in a Moment* sign. She unwound the scarf from her neck in the hot room and was growing restless when, after a few minutes, a white-haired woman approached the desk. She was carrying a shirt-sized box at her side.

"Keep watch for me, will you, miss?" the woman asked.

Carol eyed her quizzically.

The woman slipped behind the desk, placed the box on the chair, and lifted the lid. She carefully unwrapped a light-blue cardigan nestled in tissue paper. "I've been coming here for years, and the librarian has had that ratty old sweater on the back of her chair the entire time." She gestured to the offending sweater with her head. "She complimented me on my sweater earlier this week. It was this very sweater," she said, holding up the light-blue cardigan. "My daughter just gave it to me for my birthday." She removed the sweater hanging on the back of the librarian's chair, replacing it with the new sweater.

"Then something funny happened to me on the very day I'd seen Janet. I was walking along West Third Street downtown, near a bank, and a five-dollar bill blew right into my hand." The woman turned to look at Carol. Her eyes shone. "Can you imagine, miss? That money was sent from God, and I knew just what I wanted to do with it. I went straight to the store where my daughter had bought my sweater, and I got one for Janet. I decided to sneak it in here when she was away from her desk and surprise her."

The woman carefully folded the old sweater and placed it on the counter behind the desk. She withdrew an envelope from her purse with the name Janet Hatcher written in a neat scroll and propped it on top of the folded sweater. The woman stepped back and smiled at the effect.

"That's terribly thoughtful of you," Carol said. "I'm sure whoever lost that money would be glad to know how it was used."

The woman turned to Carol. "I never thought of that. You could be right. At any rate, I'm going to skedaddle. If she sees me here, she'll know and probably try to give the sweater back."

"Won't she know that it's you when she reads the note?"

The woman shook her head. "I signed it Santa Claus." She squeezed Carol's arm as she stepped around the desk.

"A very merry Christmas, my dear," the woman said.

"And to you," Carol replied as the woman hurried to the exit.

⁂

Carol watched until the door closed behind the woman. She was turning back to the desk when she caught sight of Janet Hatcher, waving to her from the side of the reading room. Carol smiled at the woman hurrying back to her station.

"Sorry to keep you waiting, Carol," Janet said. "I was helping the nicest boy select a biography for a book report." She removed the sign from the front of her desk. "Now, what can I do for you?"

Carol slid her mother's list across the desk. "My mother would like me to pick up books on these topics. Can you help me find the right ones?"

"I'm sure I can," Janet said, replacing her glasses on her nose as she studied the paper. She sat back in her high chair and reached for her sweater. She began absent-mindedly pulling it around her shoulders, then stopped abruptly. She let the list fall to her desk when she realized it was not her familiar sweater. "What in the world?!" she cried as she brought the soft garment onto her lap. She turned it over in her hands and looked at Carol, wide-eyed.

"It's lovely," Carol said.

"It certainly is," Janet said. "But it's not my sweater. Did you see who left it here?"

Carol drew a deep breath. "I did." She pointed to the note lying on top of the folded sweater on the counter behind the desk. "Santa Claus."

Janet swiveled in her chair and ran her hand over the top of her old sweater. She opened the envelope and withdrew a small handwritten note. A smile played on the corners of her mouth. She turned back to Carol.

"I know who left this," she said. "And it wasn't Santa Claus. It was an older woman with a shock of white hair, wasn't it?"

Carol shrugged. "It might have been."

"That was very thoughtful of her, but I can't accept this. I'll give it back the next time I see her," she said, slipping into her old sweater.

"She wants you to have it," Carol protested. "She was so pleased to give it to you. She'd been hanging around, waiting for you to leave your desk so she could slip it over your chair. Don't spoil it for her. Wear it and enjoy it."

"It is beautiful," Janet said, fingering the fine yarn as she folded it carefully. "But she's on a limited budget, like me. She can't afford this. I complimented her on the same sweater when she wore it a few days ago. Her daughter gave it to her for her birthday. She didn't buy it for herself, and I can't let her buy one for me."

"I think she can afford it," Carol said.

The librarian raised her eyebrows.

"She told me she found a five-dollar bill on the street that day. She used it to buy the sweater."

"And you believed her? That she found money on the street?"

"I know she's telling the truth," said Carol. "I was on the same stretch of sidewalk Monday when a woman fell and dropped six five-dollar bills. The wind took them away and apparently this woman found one of them. She told me that the money was a gift from God and that the first thing she thought to do with it was to buy you this sweater." Carol paused and looked into Janet's eyes. "She thinks God wants you to have that blue sweater. So do I."

Janet swallowed hard. "If that's really what happened … But what about the woman who lost her money?" She turned quizzical eyes to Carol.

Carol assured her with the story of a kind stranger who'd secretly pulled a stack of bills from his wallet and presented it to Verna Lind as the "found" Christmas money. In the retelling, she omitted her own contribution to Verna's fund, knowing Janet would want to repay her.

"What a wonderful man, and what a lovely Christmas miracle."

"Isn't it?" Carol sighed, thinking of Edward Fuller. "Then I guess I'd better put this on and enjoy it."

Carol beamed. "I think you must."

Janet drew the sweater around her shoulders and picked up Carol's list. "Follow me," she said, getting out of her chair. "I've got just what you need over here."

Carol Clark was hidden behind a row of shelves in the history section when Edward Fuller and Stanley Parker crossed the reading room, checked out two biographies, and headed for the movie theater.

# *Chapter 8*

Donna Jorgensen counted out change into the open palm of the man on the other side of the perfume counter. She handed him his parcel, neatly dressed in the Christmas paper that was Higbee's signature holiday wrap this season. "Thank you, sir. Merry Christmas," she said as he turned away.

It was the last Saturday before Christmas so she'd expected to be busy, but the crowds in the store surprised her. Customers two to three deep lined the retail counters as far as she could see. If she stood on her tiptoes and leaned to the right, she could view a portion of the escalator carrying flocks of people to the upper floors. It had been working at capacity all day. If this kept up, she wouldn't be able to purchase the stockings that were on sale on the third floor during her break. She'd never get waited on in time to return to her post at the perfume counter.

Donna had wanted a pair of those stockings with the embroidered design at the heel seam—a pair of genuine Harlequin heels—since she'd seen them in the movie magazines that her sister brought home from the beauty shop.

She had the money to buy both her sister and herself a pair. They lived at home and turned their paychecks over to their mother, who gave them each a modest allowance. One that didn't allow such luxuries as a pair of Harlequin heels. Donna smiled. She had a secret source of funds. They'd wear the fashionable stockings to the Sunday afternoon Christmas dance at their church.

"Miss, can you help me?" came the agitated voice of a stocky man stabbing his chubby finger at the glass counter.

"So sorry, sir," she said, stepping to him. "How may I be of assistance?"

"My wife always likes this stuff," he said.

"Arpege?" Donna asked.

"That's it," he replied. "Give me a bottle of that."

"Would you like the perfume or the cologne?"

"Geez. I have no idea. What'd you think?"

"I'd go with the perfume, sir," she replied. "It's more expensive, but it's our best seller and the most popular gift."

The man nodded. "That'll do. Can you wrap it up quick?" He made a show of glancing at this watch. "I've got somewhere I have to be."

"Certainly, sir," she said, trying to squelch her irritation. "Which size do you prefer?" She gave him the prices.

"That much?"

Donna nodded.

"Better give me the smallest bottle," he said as he reached into his wallet.

Donna removed a small bottle of Arpege perfume from the drawer below the display case and quickly wrapped it for the customer. Like the man before him, he collected his change and purchase in silence and turned his back on her without as much as a thank you. She was about to turn her attention to a woman perusing the display to her left when she noticed a small boy at the end of the counter. He stood stock still, hands clasped, large round eyes trained on her.

"I'll be with you in a moment," she said to the woman and approached the boy. On closer inspection, he appeared to be a bit older than she had thought—maybe eleven or twelve—but small for his age. "May I help you, young man?" she asked. His shirt collar was frayed and the fingers of his gloves were almost worn through. *Hand-me-down clothes, without a doubt,* she thought. He certainly wouldn't be able to afford anything in one of her cases. She ought to run him off quickly and turn her attention back to customers who could afford the merchandise.

"I'd like to buy a present for my mother," he said. "She's never had perfume but the lady she works for wears it, and Mom's always talking about it." He squared his shoulders. "I'm here to buy perfume for my mom."

Donna suppressed a smile. "Perfume isn't just one thing, you know. It comes in a lot of different fragrances. Do you know what your mother likes?"

A cloud drifted across the boy's face. "No. She's always talking about number five," he said. "The lady that she keeps house for wears number five."

"Ah ... that would be Chanel No. 5," Donna said. "We've got it right over here." She led him to a display counter featuring the iconic fragrance. "It's one of our most expensive perfumes," she warned. "Maybe you'd like to go to the dime store to look for something for your mother.

It'll still be lovely and much more affordable. You could find something with a similar bottle," she said kindly.

The boy shook his head emphatically. "No. I want her to have what that lady has."

Donna scanned the counter and noted four people waiting for her attention. She'd tried to be kind to this boy, but she really should tell him she couldn't help him and get back to paying customers. She opened her mouth to tell him to move along, but something about the set of his jaw stopped her. "How much money do you have?"

The boy laid a large cloth bag on the counter and untied the string holding it shut. He turned the bag on its side and carefully slid out a small mountain of coins. "I'm a paperboy," he said. "I've been saving my tips all year. I've got a good route and there's a lot of money here."

Donna inwardly groaned. "Do you know how much?"

The boy nodded solemnly. "I have eight dollars and ten cents," he said proudly.

"I'm sorry," she said gently, "the cheapest item in the No. 5 line is twelve dollars." She turned to a customer who was sidling next to the young boy. "I'll be with you as soon as I finish with this customer," she said primly. Donna turned back to the boy, who stood, head down, running his hands through the money spread out on the counter. "Maybe you'd like to look at another fragrance?"

He shook his head. "I want her to have what she wants for once." He started scooping coins from the pile on the counter and placing them in the bag.

The customer standing next to the boy leaned over the counter and began to speak. "I'd like to see one of the items …" Donna held up her hand to stop him.

"Let me see if any of the Chanel No. 5 perfumes are on sale," she told the boy. He stopped gathering up his coins and lifted hopeful eyes to hers. "I'll be right back," she said.

Donna took a deep breath as she stepped into the cash register area in the middle of the display counters. She bent down and took her purse from the bottom drawer and removed the five-dollar bill tucked neatly inside her wallet. The same bill that had blown into her hands as she walked into the wind along the Public Square on her way to work earlier that week. At first, she thought a piece of paper had blown out of one of the overflowing trash cans, as sometimes happened. She hadn't believed her good fortune.

Donna hadn't given the five-dollar bill to her mother. She planned to spend it on the Harlequin heel stockings, with a little left over for ice cream after the dance. Donna hesitated, then slipped the five-dollar bill into her pocket. She and her sister would go to the dance tomorrow without Harlequin heel stockings. There were more important uses for this money.

Donna approached the boy. He swallowed noticeably and turned solemn eyes to hers.

She smiled broadly. "This is your lucky day, young man. We had one bottle of the sale perfume left. You've got just enough. Shall I gift wrap it for you?"

# Chapter 9

The church reception hall was filled with young men in Sunday suits and polished shoes and girls sporting the paper-doll look, wearing their five-yard skirts over thick-net petticoats. The disc jockey was playing "Tell Me Why" by Eddie Fisher and Hugo Winterhalter. Donna Jorgensen smiled at her partner as the song drew to a close. He made no move to release her hand as she took a step back. "Will you excuse me?" she asked. "I'd like to powder my nose."

He reluctantly let her go. "Will you dance with me again?" he called to her as she moved away.

Donna smiled at him over her shoulder and nodded. She wound her way through the crowded dance floor as the next number began to play and spotted her sister on the other side of the room. Sarah was making her way off the floor, too. Donna caught Sarah's eye and pointed to the ladies' room.

The sisters met at the white door bearing a large *W* and stepped into the room together. The powder room was full of young women touching up their lipstick and gossiping about the men in attendance. A haze of hair spray hung in the air. Donna squeezed into a spot at the mirror next to a woman wearing a red coat with fur collar and cuffs. The woman was arranging her thick chestnut hair into a chignon at the nape of her neck.

"Having fun?" Sarah asked her sister, turning to the mirror and pulling her compact out of her purse.

Donna hugged herself. "I sure am. That guy I was dancing with seems very nice," she said. "He wants to dance with me again."

Sarah smiled at her sister. "Good. And I'm not surprised. You look absolutely stunning."

Donna surveyed herself in the mirror. "You did a fabulous job with my hair," she said, turning her head side to side. "That rinse you put on it makes it look exactly like Maureen O'Hara's. I think I actually like my red hair now. I appreciate that you always style it for me before we go out. I wish I could thank you."

"What are you talking about?" Sarah asked. "You always thank me."

"I mean a proper thank you," Donna replied. "In fact, I was going to get you—each of us, actually—a pair of those Harlequin heel stockings you like so much."

"What? You can't afford those! Mama would never let you keep the money you'd need to buy those."

"I know. I had another plan ..." Donna began.

The woman in the red coat dropped her arms to her sides and blew out her breath in frustration. Her chignon sagged onto her shoulders in a tangled mass of hairpins.

"Can I help you with that?" Sarah asked the woman, reaching up to assist without waiting for an answer. "I'm a beautician," she added. "You look familiar. Do you come to these dances often?"

"This is my first one. I've just started singing in the choir. Maybe that's where you've seen me."

"That must be it," Sarah said. "What's your name?"

"Carol Clark."

"I'm Sarah Jorgensen. And this is my sister, Donna," she said as she removed hairpins from their perch in Carol's hair and placed them between her teeth.

Carol smiled at her. "You're obviously much better at this than I am, Sarah," she said. "I'd be grateful."

Sarah raised an eyebrow at her sister. "So what was your plan?" she said through her teeth as she began winding Carol's thick hair into a coil.

"I found a five-dollar bill this week," Donna said.

Carol fastened her gaze on Donna's reflection in the mirror.

"Where?" Sarah gasped.

"On the street. I was on my way back to the store. I had my head down, walking into the wind. The bill blew into my hands. At first I thought it was a piece of trash, but it was a five-dollar bill."

"You never mentioned it."

"I know. I didn't want Mama to take it from me. I was going to get us each a pair of stockings and have money left over for ice cream after the dance. It was meant to be a surprise."

"So what happened? Did you feel guilty and tell Mama?"

Donna shook her head. "I waited on the sweetest boy yesterday at the store. He wanted to buy his mother Chanel

No. 5 for Christmas and had saved every cent of his paper route money all year."

Sarah snorted. "It'd take more than that to buy Chanel No. 5."

"He was almost five dollars short of what he needed, so I got the bill out of my wallet and added it to his money so he could buy the perfume. I acted like it was on sale."

"That was really nice of you," Sarah said. She inserted the last hairpin into Carol's smooth chignon and stood back to admire her work.

"There was something so genuine and caring about this boy. He said his mother worked for a lady who wore No. 5. I'm guessing his mother is a cook or cleaning woman. He said his mother was always talking about the perfume the lady wore. I couldn't stop myself from helping him."

"I'd have done the same thing. We don't need those stupid Harlequin heels. We've got men swarming us as it is." She squeezed her sister's arm. "I'm proud of you."

Carol cleared her throat. "What day was that, do you remember?"

"Tuesday. Early afternoon," Donna replied. "Why do you ask?"

"You're not going to believe this," Carol said and told them about the lady at the bank. "I'll bet you ended up with one of those five-dollar bills."

"I was only a block from there," Donna said. "You must be right." She looked at Carol. "Should I give the money back to you? Or that kind man?"

Carol shook her head emphatically. "Of course not. I'm delighted that you gave the boy that money. I got the man's name but I have no idea how to contact him," she said, unable to conceal the note of disappointment in her voice.

"I feel like I owe you the money," Donna persisted, "since you chipped in that much to help the old woman."

"Nonsense," Carol stated firmly. "Your sister, here, has done a brilliant job with my hair," she said, smiling at Sarah. "I say we call it even." Carol patted her now stylish chignon.

"Glad you like it," Sarah said. "I work at a shop around the corner." She handed Carol a card. "In case you ever need another updo."

Carol tucked the card into her purse.

"So what happened to the man? You sounded sad when you mentioned him. He must have been awfully nice."

Carol sagged against the wall. "To be truthful, I've been thinking of him nonstop ever since we met. There was something about him."

"What did he look like?"

"Tall and handsome; in his early thirties, I'd guess. He wore glasses and carried a heavy briefcase. He's probably a businessman or an attorney."

"Did he seem interested in you?" Sarah asked with the interrogation skills of an experienced beautician.

"That's the thing—I thought he was. And we exchanged names," she said.

"Carol Clark is a common name," Donna observed. "Maybe he's having trouble finding you. Cleveland is a big city."

Carol groaned. "I hadn't thought of that."

"Maybe you'll run into him again," Donna said. "What do you do? Do you work?"

"I'm a stenographer," Carol replied. "I work for a law firm."

"There you are, then," Sarah exclaimed. "Maybe he'll come into your office on business."

Carol shrugged. "That seems like a long shot."

"If it's meant to be, you'll see him again. Mark my words," Sarah said. "Now let's get back to the dance floor. I'm not going to meet any men by standing around in the ladies' room."

&

Carol hung her coat in the cloakroom and spotted her coworker swirling around on the dance floor. Jean had been after her for months to join her at one of the church's Sunday afternoon dances. Meeting Edward Fuller had awakened her desire to be part of a couple again. She'd been alone long enough. It was time.

She sidled along the wall and was about to sink onto a folding chair when someone tapped her on the shoulder from behind. She turned and was met with the shining face of a young man fully six inches shorter—and at least ten years younger—than herself. He held out his hand and she smiled.

"I should warn you that I'm quite rusty," she said, raising her voice to be heard above the music. "I haven't been dancing in almost a decade."

"You're in the right hands then," he said. "I'm easily the best dancer in the room—male or female."

Carol raised her eyebrows, and the man smiled.

"I'm Jim Parker," he said as he took her hand and led her to the dance floor. "You can judge for yourself."

Jim Parker was, indeed, an excellent dancer and a superb partner. Carol followed his lead and soon found herself executing dips and spins as if she'd just completed a dance class.

"You're really good," he complimented her between numbers. "Surely you must have gone dancing sometime during the last ten years."

"Sadly, no," Carol shook her head. "My last dance was with my fiancé before he left for the Pacific."

Jim looked into her eyes and waited.

"He was killed, and I haven't danced with anyone since." Her voice caught, and she turned her head aside.

"I'm sorry," he said.

Carol nodded and turned back to him. "You mustn't let me monopolize your time. I'm sure the other girls here are dying to dance with you. Girls your own age, too." She smiled at him and stepped back. "I really should be going, anyway."

Jim Parker caught her hand. "I want you to stay and dance with me," he said. "That is, if you're having fun. I'm having a great time." He motioned to the crowd with his head. "You wouldn't believe the number of girls who won't dance with a short guy like me. So you'd be doing me a favor."

Carol laughed. "That's their loss, I'm afraid. If you're game, so am I."

"When the dance is over, I can give you a ride. My uncle is picking me up in his car, and we'll see you safely home."

"How could I refuse such a kind offer?" For the first time since that dreadful day when she'd learned of Ken's death, Carol Clark forgot her sorrow and loneliness and had a good time.

∽∽∞∽∽

Edward Fuller pulled his automobile to the curb outside the church where his 19-year-old nephew was attending a dance. He opened the Sunday *Plain Dealer* that he'd brought with him and turned to the editorial section.

He finished the column he was reading and checked his watch. The dance should be over. Groups of young people were exiting the church, jostling and joking; everyone with rosy cheeks and high spirits. Maybe one of these days he would take Jim's advice and go to the dance, too. It looked like everyone had had fun. He rubbed his hands together. The setting sun had slipped behind the church, leaving his car in deep shadow. He was getting cold.

Edward got out of his car. If he knew Jim, he was involved in deep conversation with a girl he'd met. At nineteen, Jim was more of a ladies' man than Edward had ever been. He'd have to go in there and drag Jim out to the car. His sister had been nice enough to invite him to stay for supper, and he wouldn't upset her by being late.

He was almost to the door when it opened and Jim Parker hurried out.

Edward smiled. "I figured I'd better come get you or we'd be late for supper and your mom would have both of our hides."

Jim nodded. "We were almost going to be even later," he said.

"How so?" Edward asked as they made their way back to his car.

"I danced with the most remarkable woman all afternoon," Jim replied. "I offered to give her a ride home after the dance and was in there trying to convince her to accept."

"Another conquest? You collect girls like trading cards."

Jim shook his head. "It wasn't like that. There's something really special about this woman. And I think she'd be perfect for you, not me."

Edward glanced at Jim as they got into the car. "Really? Why do you think she'd be perfect for me?"

"She's the right age, for one thing, and she's classy and smart. And a real looker. Plus she's in your field—she's a stenographer."

"You don't say? So where is this woman?"

"She's getting a ride home from a gal she works with, the one who convinced her to come to the dance." Jim turned his attention to his side window, then tugged on Edward's arm as he began to pull away from the curb. "There she is, now," he said.

Edward leaned forward to look where Jim was pointing and caught a glimpse of a woman in a familiar red coat stepping into a car. He turned sharply to Jim. "The woman in the red coat with the dark hair?"

Jim nodded.

Edward took a deep breathe. "Did you get her name?"

Jim Parker rolled his eyes. "Of course I got her name. Carol Clark."

# Chapter 10

Verna Lind glanced at the door as the bell tinkled, announcing a new customer. She brushed aside the strand of hair that had escaped her tight bun and smiled at the familiar man in the heavy tweed overcoat. Howard Hamlin came into the bakery every weekday morning at precisely seven forty-five. He purchased two glazed doughnuts and tucked his newspaper and bakery bag under his arm, then walked the three blocks to his office in downtown Cleveland.

The bakery was busy in the mornings and Verna didn't have much time to chat with customers, but over the past year she'd learned his name, that he was a probate attorney, and that his wife had died some time ago. She had suspected that he was a widower since he never ate breakfast at home.

"Good morning, Mr. Hamlin. We've got a chilly one today, haven't we? I've got some lovely banana-nut muffins, fresh out of the oven, if you'd like a change," she said, knowing that he would stick with his regular order.

"No thank you, Verna," Howard said. "I'll have the usual."

Verna nodded and retrieved the paper sack that she had waiting for him behind the counter. "Right you are, then." She handed him the bag as he passed the requisite amount to her. She caught his eye and smiled at him. "I'm going to keep asking you. Who knows—one of these days you may surprise me."

Howard flushed and looked at his shoes. "I guess I'm a creature of habit."

"Nothing wrong with that," she said, sorry that her kidding had embarrassed him. "I eat the same thing almost every night for dinner."

Howard cocked an eyebrow at her.

"I broil a piece of bread topped with a slice of cheese. By the time my son and I close up here, that's all I have the energy to fix."

"Why don't the two of you eat out after work?"

Verna sighed and leaned against the counter. "He's got a wife and three young boys to get home to and can't spare the time. I don't fancy eating alone."

Howard nodded in agreement. "I haven't eaten in a restaurant since my wife died, unless it was for business."

"If I had the chance—and the money—I'd take myself for a meal at the Stahler House whether I was alone or not. I ate there once, and it was heavenly." She swept his face with eyes the color of aquamarines, then patted the counter as another customer pushed through the door. "One day, I'm going to go back there."

Howard pivoted as Verna turned her attention to the next customer. The Stahler House. It had been their favorite spot when Edith was alive. He'd like to go back there. It'd be fun to take Verna Lind there, he thought and instantly regretted it. How could he think such a thing? He hurried out the door and stepped briskly toward his office.

Howard picked his way gingerly across the icy parking lot to the entrance of the restaurant. He reached for the ornate iron handle on the door and paused. The last time he'd been inside, he'd been celebrating his thirty-fifth wedding anniversary. That was now five long years ago and Edith had been gone more than four of those years.

The Stahler House made the best steaks and chops in town and no one could touch their apple pie a la mode. It was silly to deny himself the pleasure of a good meal, he told himself. Lots of people ate alone in restaurants. Wasn't that young attorney at his firm always recommending places where he'd dined alone? If Edward Fuller could do it, so could he. His self-imposed boycott had gone on long enough. It was time to get on with the business of living.

A strong gust of wind pushed him backward. He resisted its force and grasped the handle, wrestling the door open. Howard stamped the snow off of his shoes and removed his gloves as he scanned the restaurant. It was early and the dining room was almost empty. He didn't recognize the maître d', but one of the waiters looked familiar and the decor was unchanged. His breath caught in his throat as his gaze rested on the table where he and Edith had been seated on their anniversary. *Maybe this wasn't such a good idea after all.*

"May I help you, sir?" said a tall man in a slim tuxedo and crisp white shirt. "Do you have a reservation?"

Howard nodded and forced himself to focus on the man. Now that he was here, he may as well go through with it. "Yes. For Hamlin," he told the man.

The maître d' ran his finger down a list in an open book on the podium and tapped one of the entries. "Very good," he said. "For one?"

The words stung like salt in an open wound. The maître d' looked at him and raised an eyebrow.

"Yes. One," Howard stammered.

"This way please."

The maître d' skirted the outside of the dining room and placed Howard at a table near the window. "You can enjoy the view here, sir," the man said, handing him a large leather-bound menu. "It's very pretty when it snows."

Howard nodded and looked into the restaurant as he sat down. He had a clear view of the table where he and Edith had celebrated and thought about asking to be moved, then decided against it. He didn't have to look at the table. He'd look out the window as the man suggested.

The waiter approached and recited the long list of the day's specials. Howard's mind had been made up since he'd made the reservation; he ordered a large porterhouse steak, medium rare.

"Would you like a glass of wine with that?" the man asked.

Howard shook his head, gesturing to himself as a lone diner.

"We've got some lovely wines by the glass."

Howard caught the man's eye. Now that he lived alone, he never bothered to open a bottle. A glass of wine would be nice. "Bring me a red, please. Whatever you have will be fine."

"I've got just the thing. It'll pair perfectly with your steak. Would you like a glass to enjoy before your salad?"

"Why not?" Howard replied. He leaned back and watched a light flurry of snow dance in front of the streetlight outside the window.

The restaurant began to fill as the maître d' seated couples out for a night on the town, and waiters passed each other, balancing large silver trays loaded with plates of food. The room buzzed with the hum of conversation.

Howard Hamlin was halfway through his second glass of wine and eating a wedge of crisp iceberg lettuce dressed with blue cheese when he noticed the maître d' escort a young couple to the table that he had been so studiously ignoring. The maître d' took the coat of the woman who was very much in a family way. The man held her chair, and Howard noticed that she wore a small corsage of white roses. He turned his head quickly toward the window and stared at his reflection in the glass.

He'd brought Edith here on their first wedding anniversary, when she'd been pregnant with Bobby. Howard swallowed and blinked hard.

"May I take your salad away, sir?" the waiter asked.

Howard nodded.

"Your steak will be right out."

Howard focused on the young, pregnant couple, all the while admonishing himself for doing so. He watched as the man leaned over the table toward the woman, pointing to something on the menu. She put her hand over her heart, and he could imagine her saying, "Really? Isn't that terribly expensive?" And the man responding, "It's our special day, and nothing's too good for you." Just like he had said to Edith in the carefree days before they'd started a family.

This young couple was on the verge of an adventure, the likes of which they couldn't imagine. They'd have their ups and downs, but if they loved each other like they did now, they could weather any storm. He and Edith had. Howard was smiling as the waiter set his entree on the table.

"Here you are, sir. I'll check back to make sure everything is to your liking."

The savory aroma of his meal tore his attention from the young couple. Howard picked up his knife and tucked into the best steak he'd had in years. When he'd finished, he leaned back in his chair and sighed. The evening hadn't been as hard as he feared it would be. Memories of Edith had been with him, to be sure, but they were happy ones. She would have been proud of him for coming out tonight, and he was proud of himself.

When the waiter cleared his plate, he ordered apple pie a la mode and coffee to finish his meal. He'd come this far, and he wasn't going to leave without a taste of that pie.

"Will there be anything else?" the waiter asked.

Howard shook his head. "Just the check."

As he was reaching into his wallet to pay his bill, he pulled out the five-dollar bill that he'd found on the street last week. It felt warm between his fingers, and he could hear Edith's voice in his head. A smile flooded his face and he gestured to the waiter.

"Something else, sir?"

"Yes. I'd like to pay the bill of that young couple over there," Howard said, gesturing to the table where the couple was being served slices of prime rib from a trolley. "The couple that's expecting."

"Do you know them?" the waiter asked.

"In a way. They remind me of my wife and me when we were their ages. I had some good fortune last week, and I'd like to do this for them," he said. He could swear he felt his wife's warm hand on his arm.

"That's very kind of you, sir," the waiter said. "I'll go let them know."

"No," Howard replied quickly. "I want this to be a surprise for them after I've gone. No need to embarrass them."

The waiter nodded. "As you wish. I hope you have a very merry Christmas, and that we see you again, soon. My name's Martin, and I'd be pleased to serve you again."

Howard rose to his feet. "A very merry Christmas to you, too, Martin. I'll be back," he said. "And next time, I'll bring a friend." He turned up the collar of his coat and slipped on his gloves before going out into the cold, quiet night. Maybe it was time he started over. Verna Lind's smiling face filled his thoughts. Maybe he'd ask for more than his usual doughnuts and coffee one of these mornings.

# *Chapter 11*

Carter Williams sat in the chair normally reserved for his shoe-shine customers and rested his elbows on the arm rests. He checked his pocket watch. It was two forty-five in the afternoon on the Monday before Christmas. He pulled his wallet out of his pocket and re-counted the bills that were neatly folded in a separate compartment. Carter smiled. With the extra five-dollar tip, he'd surely have enough money.

Carter surveyed the main concourse of Terminal Tower. Pedestrian traffic was light. He'd be able to make his purchase and be back in time for the late-afternoon rush. He picked up his sign that announced *Back In*, with an arrow to a clock, and set it for four o'clock. He placed the sign in the chair and set off across the concourse with purpose.

Carter was headed for Higbee's. He was certain they'd have the gift he'd been saving for; the one that had him coming in early and staying late to assure he'd have the necessary funds.

Carter consulted the store directory and took the escalator to the floor indicated for *Women's Coats*. He was going to get his sister a new coat for Christmas; a red coat with fur collar and cuffs, like the one worn by that pretty brunette he saw walking through the concourse almost every day. The brunette had a certain presence about her, like his sister used to have before life beat her down.

Things were going well for his sister and her three boys until her husband fell off a fifteen-foot ladder. Her husband was unable to continue to work as a carpenter, and her family was barely making ends meet. He'd offered to help with food and rent, but both his sister and her husband were too proud to accept.

Carter understood how demoralizing it could be to live hand-to-mouth, with never enough to get by. His sister's coat was a shabby hand-me-down that should have been relegated to the rag bag years ago. He'd give her something luxurious and stylish to make her feel pretty and remind her who she really was.

He made his way to the proper department and stopped short when he saw the racks that stretched before him; neat rows of coats in every color and description. He stood at the edge of the displays, unsure where to begin.

A slender woman in an austere black suit and sensible shoes approached him. "May I help you, sir?"

Carter released the breath he'd been holding. "Thank you. I'm here to buy a coat. For my sister."

The woman smiled. "We have some lovely tweeds over here," she said, moving toward a rack to her left. "Very warm and sensible."

Carter shook his head. "I want a red coat with a fur collar and cuffs."

The woman raised an eyebrow.

"Do you have anything like that?"

"Right this way," she said. "They're beautiful and will make a lovely gift."

Carter followed as she wound her way through the crowded department, bringing him to a rack that held two coats. They were a rich lipstick red and the collar and cuffs were trimmed in warm brown fir.

"That's it!" he cried. "That's exactly what I want." He stepped to the rack and removed one of the coats on its hanger. He turned it over in his hand, admiring the elegant garment.

"That's mink," the saleslady said. "That's a very fine coat."

Carter cut his eyes to her. He'd heard of mink, knew it was expensive. He reached for the price tag with an unsteady hand.

"That coat will be on sale on the day after Christmas," the woman said. "Perhaps you'd rather wait?"

Carter shook his head. It would take everything he'd saved, plus a little from his monthly spending money, but he had enough. "The twenty-sixth won't do. I want it for Christmas."

"This is a most generous gift. Your sister is very lucky to have such a kind and generous brother. And one with such good taste."

Carter flushed.

"Do you know what size she wears?"

He shook his head. "She's about your size—maybe a little taller. What would you wear?"

"You're in luck," the woman said. "I'm a six, and this one here," she said, pulling a coat off the rack, "is the last six in stock."

She motioned for him to follow her to the register. "May I gift wrap this for you?"

Carter paid for his purchase and took the beautifully-wrapped box back to his shoe-shine stand. He placed it behind the chair and made sure that it was out of sight.

He'd just removed the sign from the chair when Mr. Rosen approached. "Hello, Carter," the man said. "By the smile on your face, I'd say you won a pot of gold."

"You know, sir, I feel as happy as if I had. I'm the luckiest person I know." He paused and looked into Mr. Rosen's eyes. "Why don't you sit down and tell me about you. How's your son doing?"

Mr. Rosen sat and poured out his story as Carter ministered to not just his scuffed shoes but his bruised soul as well.

# Chapter 12

Larisa Denisovich sighed as she heard the door to her shop open. She quickly secured the last two stitches in the seam she was repairing and set the pair of tuxedo slacks on her work table. Larisa glanced at the clock on the wall as she made her way through the curtain that separated her workroom from her small lobby. With any luck, she'd finish the repair before the end of the day.

She smiled at the red-headed man who was leaning one elbow on the tall counter. "Mr. Park. Your wife's dress is ready." She turned to a long rod that ran the width of the room and found the hanger holding the sequined gown that she had labored long and hard to shorten. "I thought she might come by to pick it up herself so that she could try it on again. Make sure it's right."

"She's a bit under the weather, so she sent me. I'm sure it'll be fine."

"I hope she feels better for Christmas," Larisa replied. "And that she can enjoy wearing this beautiful dress. It's one of the prettiest things I've ever worked on."

"She's planning to wear it when we go out on New Year's Eve. I'm sure she'll be better by then." Tony reached into his pocket and took out his wallet. "Did you get your Christmas tree?" he asked, trying to sound nonchalant.

"Oh, Mr. Park, we certainly did." Larisa handed him a receipt. "You won't believe what happened."

Tony nodded encouragingly.

"The proprietor from the tree lot where we ran into you brought us a tree after he closed down that night."

Tony arched his brows.

"It had lights and decorations on it already. It's so beautiful—you've never seen a prettier tree." Larisa's eyes shone. "He said it was a sample tree and nobody wants to buy a decorated tree. He told me he had sold almost every tree he had and would be closing the lot by the weekend. He planned to throw the decorated tree in the dumpster but then he remembered Sasha and me. He thought we might be able to use it so he dropped it off at our apartment last Thursday night."

"That was nice of him," Tony remarked.

"It was so nice. He said we were doing him a big favor, but I know he was the one doing us a favor." She shook her head. "You should have seen the look on my daughter's face. And Sasha's." Larisa brought her hands to the sides of her face. "He was so excited he ran around and around the tree."

"I'm very happy to hear it, Mrs. Denisovich. You deserve something nice."

Larisa blushed and looked away. "I took the man a full batch of pastilas to thank him." She turned back to him. "You know pastilas?"

Tony shook his head no.

Larisa patted his hand. "You need to know. Wait," she commanded him.

She rushed into the workroom and returned with a small paper sack containing a few of the treats. "There's good luck in every one." She placed the sack into his hands. "Merry Christmas, Mr. Park."

# Chapter 13

Edward Fuller took off his glasses and rubbed his hand over his eyes. The motion he was drafting would need another couple of hours of work. He sat back in his chair and noticed the absence of any sound outside his door. He checked his watch; it was almost three o'clock on Christmas Eve. The office had officially closed for business at two.

The motion would have to wait. He needed to head to his sister's for dinner, followed by the Christmas Eve service at church. It was his job to corral his nephews so his sister could arrive early to warm up with the choir.

He removed his hat and coat from the hook on the back of his door and headed for the lobby. Rosemary Payne was fumbling with the cantankerous old lock on the double doors as he entered.

"Here—let me help you with that," he said. She stepped aside and he wrestled with the dead bolt until it clicked open. "What are you still doing here?" he asked. "We closed up an hour ago."

Rosemary cast him a sidelong glance. "Mr. Hamlin had a few things he needed me to finish up."

Edward shook his head. "Doing his Ebenezer Scrooge impression?" He sighed. "We don't want that. Don't you have somewhere to be?"

Rosemary nodded as he held the door for her. "I'm catching a train to Pittsburgh at four."

"Is he still back there?" Edward asked, gesturing with his thumb.

"Yes. He told me he didn't have any plans and would be working late. Said he gets a lot done when it's quiet."

"Yes ... well ... we'll see about that. Merry Christmas to you, Miss Payne."

She picked up the small satchel that she'd dropped at her feet while she was struggling with the lock. "And to you, Mr. Fuller," she said as she stepped through the door.

He locked the door behind her and proceeded down the corridor to Howard Hamlin's office. Working late on Christmas Eve? He didn't think so.

Howard Hamlin started at the sound of the knock on his door. He glanced over the top of his half-moon glasses and smiled at his young law partner outlined in the doorway. Howard wasn't an outgoing type and didn't have a wide social circle but counted Edward Fuller as one of his few friends.

"Ah ... Edward. You're still here, too?"

Edward pointed to his hat and coat. "Just leaving. It's Christmas Eve, you know. Knocking off at three isn't a crime."

Howard sighed. "I know. But spending the evening at home doesn't appeal to me. I may as well stay here and work."

Edward nodded. "I understand. The idea sounds attractive to me, too. But I have to go to my sister's for dinner and then take my nephews to church. She leaves early because she sings in the choir."

"That sounds nice," Howard offered.

Edward began to back out of the doorway, then stopped. "Why don't you come with me? Give a friend some support?"

"I couldn't intrude upon your sister like that. She won't want an extra guest for dinner."

"Nonsense," Edward said. "She's a terrific cook and always makes more than enough. There'll be plenty."

Howard leaned back into his chair and turned aside.

"It's Christmas Eve, Howard. You don't really want to be here. Get your coat and come with me. You'll have a good meal, and we'll go to church. I can drive you home when it's over. I'll enjoy your company, and I think you'll have fun."

Howard replaced the cap on his fountain pen and laid it carefully on his desk. He sighed heavily as he rose from his chair. "You're right; I don't want to work late tonight." He cut his eyes to his friend. "If you're sure your sister won't mind?"

Edward beamed. "Positive. The only thing that will upset my sister is if we're any later than we're already going to be."

# Chapter 14

Art Burkowski whistled as he stepped onto the platform of the train station. The train bound for Pittsburgh had arrived on time and the stationmaster would be calling "all aboard" any minute. He'd finally be going home for Christmas. Art reached into the inside breast pocket of his heavy overcoat and checked his ticket—his first-class ticket—and smiled. He'd worked sixteen straight hours on Monday and Tuesday, covering shifts at the hospital pharmacy for coworkers who had called in sick. A deluxe sleeper berth was exactly what he needed right now.

Someone grabbed his elbow from behind, and he turned to face a portly man sporting a full white beard. The man was carrying a red velvet sack trimmed in white satin. "Have you been a good boy this year?" the man asked. "I'm sure you have," he continued without waiting for Art to answer. The man reached into his sack and handed Art a candy cane.

Two adolescent boys raced up to the man. He dipped into his sack and handed them each a candy cane before he continued to weave his way through the crowd.

Art turned to survey his fellow passengers. A family of five wore matching red scarves and Santa hats. An elderly woman clutched a brightly wrapped package to her side. Everyone appeared to be in a jovial mood except for a young woman shifting her weight from one foot to the other as she tried to comfort the infant who wailed inconsolably in her arms.

Art stepped closer to the woman as the baby, swaddled in a blue blanket, swiped his hand across his ear and let out a deafening cry. The woman turned slightly, and he could see that the baby's cheeks were bright red. The signs of an ear infection were unmistakable.

The woman caught his eye. "I'm doing the best I can," she snapped. "He was fine this morning."

"I'm sure you are," he replied. "I'm a pharmacist, and I was just concerned. That's all."

She sighed heavily as she continued to jostle her baby. "I'm sorry. I shouldn't have been rude to you." She gestured to the other people on the platform with her head. "Everyone's giving me the evil eye because my baby won't stop crying. No one wants to be near us."

"I'm sure that's not true," Art said. "Have you been to see the doctor?"

The woman shook her head. "We're going to my mother's in Pittsburgh. She'll know what to do."

"He may have an ear infection," Art replied.

"Why do you say that?"

"He's in pain and was pulling at his ear earlier—that, and a fever, are telltale signs."

"Then he's got an ear infection, all right. What do I do about it?"

"He'll most likely get better on his own. When you get on the train, why don't you have the porter bring you a warm washcloth to hold over his ear? That should ease some of the pain."

The woman nodded. "Thank you. I'll do that when I get to my mother's. The porter only comes to take your ticket in third class."

Art considered the woman thoughtfully, then reached into the pocket of his coat. "I've got an idea," he said, withdrawing his first-class ticket. "Why don't we trade? You two will be much more comfortable in first class."

The woman looked at him incredulously. "I couldn't," she said. "You don't even know me."

"It's Christmas," Art said. "I insist." He picked up her suitcase and motioned for her to follow him. "They'll be boarding soon. Come with me."

Art claimed his seat in the third-class compartment. He'd helped settle the grateful mother and crying baby in what would have been his sleeper berth. He'd given the porter detailed instructions for preparing a poultice for the baby and retreated as the mother gushed her thanks.

He nestled his suitcase beneath his feet and rested his hat on his knee. The seats in the third-class compartment were cramped, but no one had come to claim the seat next to him. With any luck, he'd be able to move his belongings to the empty seat and stretch out.

The porter moved through the car, collecting tickets. Art checked his watch; they'd be departing any minute. He glanced out the window to the platform and saw a young woman with a mane of blond hair flying wildly behind her shoving her way through the crowd, waving at the train.

"Looks like you got lucky, sir," the porter said. "Somebody missed their train." He pointed to the empty seat.

"I'm not so sure." Art motioned to the woman who was now running the last few feet to the door.

"Well, sir, if I was you, I'd rather have a beautiful woman like that sitting next to me the whole way to Pittsburgh than have that empty seat."

Art flushed. He'd been thinking the same thing. He reached into his coat pocket and handed the porter his ticket as Rosemary Payne stepped into the car and made a beeline for the empty seat next to him.

Art rose and helped her settle herself into her seat.

"Gosh, I almost missed this train," she said. She leaned back in her seat, recovering her breath. "If I'd have missed this train, my mother would never have forgiven me."

"You made it—that's all that matters," Art said.

Rosemary nodded. "I worked late and didn't think it would take me so long to get to the station. I couldn't find a cab and ended up walking." She patted her hair. "I must look a sight."

"On the contrary," Art said. "You look lovely." He extended his hand. "I'm Art Burkowski."

"Rosemary Payne," she said, pulling off her glove and placing her smooth, warm hand into his. Their eyes met, and Art Burkowski was immediately grateful that he was on this train, next to Rosemary Payne. "Tell me about this job that would make you work late on Christmas Eve," Art said, all traces of fatigue vanishing.

Rosemary flashed a brilliant smile. "I've got a sandwich in my valise," she said. "Are you hungry? Why don't we share it?"

Art pulled the candy cane out of his pocket. "And I can furnish dessert."

# Chapter 15

Nancy Parker was delighted that her brother had brought his law partner to dinner. She'd made more than enough meatloaf, mashed potatoes, and green beans, and was happy to set an extra place at her table.

"Mr. Hamlin," she said as they were clearing the plates. "I'd like to ask one favor." She smiled at her brother.

"After a delicious meal like this—anything, Mrs. Parker."

"Would you see to it that my brother waits in the vestibule after the service? There's someone I want him to meet, and I don't want him racing out the door like he does every Sunday."

"I don't race out the door," Edward protested. "I'm taking Stanley and Jim back home."

"That's your excuse," Nancy said. "The boys can wait an extra half-hour." She turned to the sink, and Howard shrugged and gave Edward a rueful smile. "You have my word on it, Mrs. Parker. We'll wait until you tell us we can leave."

⁂

Verna Lind secured the deadbolt to the door of the bakery and turned the sign from *Open* to *Closed*. The morning had been frantic with customers picking up their orders of pies, cakes, and the bakery's signature yuletide danish. Now, in midafternoon, the stream of customers had slowed to a trickle. She'd sent her son home to his family at noon. They'd had a very good day, and she'd earned the right to close early.

Verna entered the room at the back of the shop where the other women were working at a feverish pace to tidy up the kitchen and bag the trash. The bakery was always left in spotless condition at the end of every day.

"Ladies, you've done enough for today. Anything else can wait until the 26th. Time to go home to your families," she said. "A very merry Christmas to you all," she told the group as they slipped into their coats and boots and exited through the rear of the shop, grateful to be on their way.

Verna was transferring the day's receipts into the safe tucked into the wall at the back of the broom closet when she thought she heard someone knocking on her front door. Verna was exhausted and wanted nothing more than to go home and take a nap. She resumed her task; whoever had come to purchase baked goods would have to purchase them somewhere else. She closed the door of the safe and spun the dial.

She had her hand on her coat when the knocking started again, more insistent this time. Verna sighed and stepped cautiously to the door, peering around the curtain that separated the kitchen from the shop. She hoped to catch a glimpse of the customer without being seen herself.

"Verna," came a familiar voice. "I can see you behind that curtain."

Verna crossed to the door. "Larisa," she said through the door. "We closed early today."

"Me, too," Larisa said.

"I'm afraid everything's put away," Verna said to the woman who ran the tailor shop two doors down from the bakery.

"I'm here to give you something," Larisa said, a shy smile playing at her lips. "Open the door." She held out an oval bundle loosely wrapped in white tissue and tied with a simple red ribbon. "It'll only take a minute."

Verna felt herself flush, embarrassed that she'd been impatient with this woman over the intrusion and that she didn't have anything to give her in return. She turned the bolt and opened the door, reaching out for Larisa's arm and drawing her inside.

"How very kind of you," she said. "You shouldn't have."

Larisa was shaking her head. "You are always so good to me. Every time I come in, you have day-old bread for me. Sometimes I think it's not really day old, is it?" She looked into Verna's eyes.

Verna looked away.

"I thought so. I made you this," she said, passing the package to Verna.

"Thank you," Verna replied. She looked at Larisa. "Shall I open it?"

"Yes, please. I hope you can use it."

Verna untied the ribbon and carefully opened the tissue. An intricately knitted wrap in shades of cream and ecru, woven with strands of gold and silver thread, fell into her hands. Verna gasped. "I've never seen a more beautiful shawl." She looked up at Larisa. "Did you knit this?"

Larisa nodded vigorously. "I was worried you wouldn't like it."

"Oh, Larisa. It would be impossible not to like this. And the fact that you made it for me makes it extra special." She looked at the woman who was now smiling broadly. "I'm not sure I have anywhere special enough to wear this."

Larisa looked startled. "You can wear it to church tonight."

"Yes, I could," Verna replied. "If I were going to church. My son and his family go with her mother on Christmas Eve. I don't like to go out at night on my own."

"Then come with me and my family," Larisa said. "My daughter drives, and we'll pick you up and bring you home. You shouldn't be alone on Christmas Eve."

Verna hesitated.

"And I'll have the pleasure of seeing you wear my shawl. Besides, I knitted blessings for you into every stitch. You'll see—it will bring you good luck," Larisa said.

Verna looked at her friend. How could she refuse such an offer? She didn't want to spend Christmas Eve alone, and it would be fun to get dressed up and wear Larisa's lovely gift. She smiled and nodded.

"Good," Larisa said. "We'll pick you up at six thirty."

Verna squeezed Larisa's hand. "Thank you. I'll be ready and waiting."

⸙

Larisa Denisovich patted her daughter's arm. "Mrs. Lind and I will save you a seat. We'll be up front."

Anna nodded. "I'll get Sasha settled in the children's room and be right back."

Larisa leaned close to Verna. "Anna is putting on a brave face, but I know she's terribly disappointed that her husband didn't make it home for Christmas. He's a merchant marine and his ship isn't scheduled to dock until day after tomorrow."

"That's a shame," Verna agreed. "Especially for Sasha."

"At least her husband will be home soon," Larisa said as they approached the usher who greeted her by name.

"The usual pew?" He asked as he led them down the long center aisle to the second row.

Verna removed her coat and folded it across her lap, adjusting her new shawl around her shoulders. She held out one end of the garment and watched the metallic threads sparkle in the light. "I've never owned something this beautiful," she whispered into Larisa's ear.

Larisa beamed. "You're a very pretty woman. You should own many lovely things. I'm so happy you like it."

The women settled back into the pew as Anna joined them.

⁂

Edward Fuller admonished his nephews to hurry. "The service is scheduled to start at any moment. We'll be lucky to find seats." He turned to Howard Hamlin. "Sorry we're so late. I'm not good at corralling these two."

Edward took the short flight of steps to the narthex two at a time. He opened the door as the first strains of the processional rang out. An usher gave them an annoyed look and took the foursome to seats in the last pew at the back of the church.

Edward placed his hat on his knees and helped his youngest nephew take off his coat while the choir proceeded down the main aisle and assumed their places in the choir loft. He searched for his sister and thought he spotted her next to a woman with long brown hair, but at this distance, he couldn't be sure.

The service began as the pastor signaled for the congregation to rise, and the organist filled the vaulted chamber with the introduction to "Joy to the World." Howard Hamlin allowed the familiar melody to wash over him and was grateful that Edward had insisted he come. He wasn't a singer so his eyes remained on the crowd while his fellow congregants took up the lyrics. A sparkling shawl at the front of the church caught his attention. And a glimpse of the wearer's delicate profile as she turned toward her neighbor sent a jolt through him. Could Verna Lind be in this church tonight?

Try though he might, leaning first to the left and then to the right, Howard was unable to catch sight of her for the remainder of the service.

The pastor gave the benediction and strode down the center aisle as the processional soared and the churchgoers filed out of the pews and trailed after him. Howard searched the faces of the people as they exited. Verna Lind passed his pew, not more than fifteen feet from him. With any luck, he'd catch up with her before she left.

He waited impatiently for his turn to leave the pew, keeping his eyes fixed on the crowd milling around the narthex as he shook the pastor's hand and wished him a merry Christmas. "I've seen someone I know; someone I'd like you to meet," he told Edward. "Do you mind if we mingle with the crowd?"

"Not at all," Edward said. "I've got to wait here, anyway, remember? My sister wants to introduce me to the most eligible woman in the choir." He rolled his eyes. "Nancy's always trying to fix me up."

Howard nodded, only half-listening to Edward as he scanned the room. He suddenly put his hand on Edward's arm. "There," he said, pointing to two women at the edge of the crowd. "Come on."

"You go ahead," Edward replied. "I'll find the boys and catch up with you."

Howard moved quickly along the edge of the crowd toward the women.

"Mrs. Lind," he said. "I thought that was you."

Verna Lind turned and her smile lit the room. "Mr. Hamlin. How nice to see you! Do you attend this church?"

"No. I'm here with a friend."

"What a coincidence. I'm here with my friend Larisa," she said, gently squeezing Larisa's forearm.

"You look lovely," he said to Verna. "We were in the back of the church and your beautiful shawl caught my eye. I wondered if it was you."

Larisa regarded them both thoughtfully and smiled.

"Larisa made this for me as a Christmas gift," Verna said, fingering the delicate knit. "I love it but told her I didn't know where I would ever wear something this nice. She invited me here tonight and told me to wear the shawl, that it would bring me luck." She looked up at him. "I'm so glad I came tonight. I enjoyed the service, and I'm happy to see you."

"Would you like another occasion to wear that shawl?" Howard asked, startled by his own boldness.

She raised an eyebrow.

"I was wondering if you'd like to join me for dinner at the Stahler House? On New Year's Eve—if you don't already have plans."

Verna drew a deep breath. *Was a man asking her out on a date after all of these years?*

Howard twisted his hat in his hand.

"I'd like that very much," Verna said.

Larisa clasped her hands to her chest. "You see? That shawl *has* brought you good luck!" The three of them began to laugh.

"I see you've found someone you know," Edward said as he and his nephews approached the trio. The two women had their backs to him.

"Let me introduce my friends," Howard said.

As Verna turned to Howard's friend, she and Edward gasped in unison. Edward extended his hand, but Verna pulled him to her for a hug.

"You know each other?" Howard asked.

Verna nodded vigorously, pulling back. "We most certainly do," she said. "Let me tell you about this real-life Prince Charming," she said as she launched into the tale of the events outside the bank. Larisa and Howard listened in quiet amazement. Howard shot Edward a look that told him he knew how Edward had really recovered Verna's money.

"Mr. Fuller didn't act alone," Verna said excitedly. "There was a woman who helped him. A very pretty young woman." She eyed Edward thoughtfully. "And she's here tonight."

"What?" Edward's head snapped up. He began frantically searching the crowd. "Where?"

"She sings in the choir," Verna said. "I'm sure that was her." She pointed to Larisa. "We were going to make our way to the choir room to see if we could find her. I wanted to say thank you again and wish her a merry Christmas. Would you like to join us?"

"I most certainly would," Edward said. "But my sister is bringing a woman from the choir over here to meet me," he said, unable to conceal the note of despair in his voice.

"I'll give her your regards—" Verna began.

"No," Edward cut her off. To his horror, he felt himself flush. "I've got to see her."

"That's the Carol Clark from the dance, isn't it?" Jim Parker asked. "You met her on the street downtown, and now she sings in the choir? Go with them," he said, pointing to Verna and Larisa, "and I'll tell Mom."

"Tell me what?" Nancy Parker asked, pushing through the crowd with her friend from the choir in tow.

Edward Fuller turned toward his sister's voice and found himself face to face with Carol Clark. Their eyes locked and, for them, everyone else disappeared.

"Carol," Nancy began, "I'd like you to meet my brother, Edward Fuller." She looked between the two of them. "You know each other?" she asked, confused.

Edward took Carol's outstretched hand and tucked it into his elbow. "We most certainly do," he said, his eyes twinkling. "I think this is my own Christmas miracle," he said. "Let me tell you how we met ..."

The End

# Thank you for reading!

If you enjoyed *The Christmas Club*, I'd be grateful if you wrote a review.

Just a few lines would be great. Reviews are the best gift an author can receive. They encourage us when they're good, help us improve our next book when they're not, and help other readers make informed choices when purchasing books. Reviews keep the Amazon algorithms humming and are the most helpful aide in selling books! Thank you.

To post a review on Amazon or for Kindle:

1. Go to the product detail page for *The Christmas Club* on Amazon.com.
2. Click "Write a customer review" in the Customer Reviews section.
3. Write your review and click Submit.

*In gratitude,*

*Barbara Hinske*

# About the Author

BARBARA HINSKE is an attorney by day, bestselling novelist by night. She inherited the writing gene from her father who wrote mysteries when he retired and told her a story every night of her childhood. She and her husband share their own Rosemont with two adorable and spoiled dogs. The old house keeps her husband busy with repair projects and her happily decorating, entertaining, cooking, and gardening. Together they have four grown children, and live in Phoenix, Arizona.

Please enjoy this sneak peek at *Coming to Rosemont* (the first novel in the *Rosemont* series):

# *Prologue*

Frank Haynes spotted the forlorn-looking creature in the trees at the side of the road. He quickly pulled his Mercedes sedan off the highway and buttoned his cashmere sport coat against the icy fog as he stepped out onto the grassy berm. He walked gingerly in his slick-bottomed dress shoes as he approached the thin calico lurking in the underbrush. The wary animal rose up on her front legs, ready to take flight, and eyed him uneasily.

Haynes crooned softly to her. He pulled his collar up against the biting wind and wished he had grabbed his topcoat out of the backseat. But he dare not move now. The cat gradually relaxed and cautiously picked her way to him over the frost-stiffened grass. The cat rubbed against his legs in the familiar figure-eight pattern and began to purr—a tiny, tentative whisper that ripened into a deep, throaty rumble.

He reached a cautious hand down to her. She stretched into him, and he knew the bond had been made. He scooped her up and cradled the filthy creature against his chest, shielding her from the cold and stroking her gently, unconcerned about his expensive coat. When she was content, he returned to his car and placed her carefully in the blanket-lined crate that lived in his backseat for just such occasions. "You're safe now," he whispered the assurance. "You won't have to worry about food or cold anymore."

He shut the mesh grate of the cage and was surprised when the cat curled up and went to sleep. Most strays meowed and screamed all the way to the no-kill shelter that Haynes had founded and currently funded.

As he slipped behind the steering wheel, Haynes automatically checked the cell phone left behind in the console and was shocked to see he missed six calls during the short time he had been rescuing the cat. All from Westbury's idiot mayor, William Wheeler. He punched the return call button as he swung back onto the highway. Wheeler picked up on the first ring.

"Frank—where have you been? All hell's going to break loose around here," Wheeler shouted into the phone.

"What's up?" Haynes replied calmly.

"The town treasurer just called and told me the town can't cover the December payments from the pension fund. We're in trouble, Frank."

*Damn*, Haynes thought. This was coming two months earlier than he predicted. They wouldn't have time to get any of the condos sold by December. "Have you talked to either of the Delgados?"

"I called Chuck to tell him to move money from the reserve account you guys told me about. He said to talk to Ron about it. Ron thinks the reserve account has been 'depleted.' Some accountant and financial advisor he is!

How did you guys let this happen? What have you been up to? If the town doesn't make those payments, we're sunk."

"Don't worry about it. I'll call Chuck and we'll get it straightened out. We always do, don't we?" Haynes disconnected the call over Wheeler's sputtering response.

*Damn this faltering real estate market and those greedy, careless Delgado brothers.* How had they drained the reserve fund so quickly? They must be siphoning money for their own use from the tidy sum that the three of them had "borrowed" from the town worker's pension fund. Fleecing the faceless public was one thing. Double-crossing Frank Haynes was quite another. Wheeler was set up to take the fall, if it came to that. He could make the trail lead to the Delgados, too. Haynes vowed to find out where every nickel had gone. He executed a sharp U-turn and headed back to Town Hall.

# Chapter 1

Maggie Martin settled herself in the back of the cab as the driver pulled away from the airport and into the thin sunshine of a late February afternoon. She nodded when he leaned back to tell her that Westbury was an hour's drive, and turned her attention to the countryside streaming by her window. She was in no mood for idle chatter with a taxi driver. The dormant farmland lay still and expectant. Occasional clumps of leafless trees were silhouetted against the storm clouds that soon filled the sky. Maggie was glad she had carefully folded and packed those extra sweaters.

She shivered in spite of the heat blasting from the vents and wondered how anyone could live in a cold climate. *Southern California might not have four seasons, but who in their right mind wanted winter?* Maggie chastised herself once again for even making this trip. She was behind in her work—she needed the billings—and she probably wouldn't find any answers, anyway.

As the monotonous scenery sped by, Maggie relived her final moments with Paul in the cardiac ICU. Wired and tubed, he was hooked up to the best equipment modern medicine had to offer. Their children, Mike and Susan, were both frantically making their way through traffic, but neither arrived in time. It had been Maggie and Paul at the very end. In his final moments, Paul rallied. He feebly squeezed

Maggie's hand and repeated breathlessly, "Sorry. So sorry. House is for you." At least, that's what she thought he said. She had been crying, and the beeping monitors and wheezing oxygen machine made it impossible to hear.

She had been over this a million times. It hadn't made any sense because she knew their house was hers. Hadn't they just paid it off and thrown a burn-the-mortgage party with the kids? She had tried to reassure Paul, to quiet him, but he had been desperate to make his point. Maggie now understood Paul's deathbed confession. That's why she had decided to come to Rosemont before she listed it for sale. She needed to get answers; to make some sense of her life.

Maggie planned to go straight to her hotel in Westbury to try to get a good night's sleep before she and the realtor toured the house and signed the listing papers the next day. But her plane had arrived forty-five minutes early, the only advantage of the bumpy flight through strong tailwinds. God knows she was exhausted, having spent another sleepless night rehashing her sham of a marriage. But she was far too curious to get a glimpse of Rosemont to wait any longer. As they passed the highway sign announcing the Westbury exit fourteen miles ahead, Maggie retrieved her house key from the zippered compartment of her purse, leaned forward, and instructed the driver to take her directly to Rosemont.

The cabbie, as it turned out, didn't need directions. "Everybody in these parts knows the place," he assured her. "It's been vacant for years," he continued as he caught her eye in his rearview mirror. "Do you know the owner?"

"I am the owner," Maggie replied with an assurance in her voice that surprised her. "Actually, I just inherited Rosemont. I'm going to put it on the market, but I'm awfully curious to see it. Since it'll still be light when we get there, I thought I'd like to see it on my own, before the realtor and I get together tomorrow."

The cabbie nodded slowly, digesting this news, as he flipped on his left-turn signal and turned into a long, tree-lined drive that wound its way up a steep hill. They rounded the final corner and Maggie gasped. At the end of a deep lawn was an elegant manor house of aristocratic proportions. Built of warm limestone, with regal multi-paned windows, a sharply pitched tile roof, and six chimneys, Rosemont had the kind of gracious good looks that never go out of style. Dazed, she handed him his fare, with a more-than-generous tip, and secured his promise to drop her luggage at her hotel and return for her in an hour.

Maggie dashed through the now falling sleet to the massive front door. The key fit smoothly into the lock but wouldn't turn. She tugged and jiggled the handle, to no effect. It wasn't moving. Maggie looked wistfully over her shoulder as the taxi took the last turn at the end of the drive and vanished beyond the trees. Why did she have to insist on coming here tonight? Impatience did her in every time.

She buttoned the top button of her coat, fished the cabbie's card out of her pocket, and unzipped her purse to retrieve her phone. She'd have to call him to come back now. It was too cold and damp outside to even walk around and look in the windows. Maggie tugged off one of her gloves with her teeth and punched in his number on her phone. She brought it to her ear and idly tried the lock one more time. She felt something shift under her hand and the sturdy lock yielded. The door creaked open. Maggie abruptly ended the call and stepped over the threshold.

Even in the gloomy light of a stormy dusk, the beauty of the house overwhelmed Maggie, and she knew, for perhaps the first time in her life, that she was home. And that nothing would ever be the same again.

The mahogany front door opened to a foyer that gave way to a generous living room. A stone fireplace with an ornately carved mantel dominated one side of the room, and a graceful stairway swept up the opposite wall to the second floor. An archway led to a room lined with bookcases. *An honest-to-goodness library, for Pete's sake,* Maggie thought.

She inched forward slowly, like a dog expecting to come to the end of its leash, and peered into the library. Although all of the furniture was draped in heavy muslin covers, the room was stunning with its six-foot-high fireplace, French doors to a patio, and a stained-glass window. "I've been transported to a movie set of an English manor house," Maggie whispered. She set her purse on a round table in the middle of the foyer and unbuttoned her coat.

The fatigue and apathy that had been Maggie's constant companions since Paul's death began to dissipate as she examined this elegant old house she had inherited. Paul had never mentioned owning an estate on fifteen acres in Westbury. At least not until his final moments. Maggie had learned there were a lot of things that Paul had never mentioned. Unlike the others, this one was a pleasant surprise.

The remainder of the first floor was comprised of a large dining room, butler's pantry, kitchen, breakfast room, laundry, maid's quarters, and a large, sunny room whose function she couldn't identify. It had a herringbone tile floor and was lined with floor-to-ceiling windows along one wall. A conservatory, maybe? *Holy cow*—did she actually own a home with a library and a conservatory? The perfect lines of the house were evident at every turn.

With mounting excitement, Maggie found the switch for the chandelier that lit the staircase and raced to the second floor. A spacious landing gave way to six separate bedroom suites. She opened the first door carefully and proceeded with increasing confidence. Each suite was lovely and distinct in its own way, with huge windows and a sitting room and bathroom for each bedroom. One had a balcony, two had fireplaces. "I actually own this place," she murmured to herself in shock. She was considering which bedroom she liked best when she thought she heard a door close below. Was it already time for the taxi to return for her? Could she possibly have been here for an hour?

Maggie tore down the stairs as surely as if she had been running down them all of her life and came face to face with a solidly built man wearing tidy work clothes. With a pounding heart but steady voice, Maggie demanded to know who he was and how he got into her house.

He stepped back and held up his hands. "I'm sorry to startle you, ma'am. I'm Sam Torres. Your realtor expected you tomorrow, and he and asked me to come by today to air the house out a bit and make sure that everything was in working order. I've been in the basement for the past three hours fiddling with the furnace. I've got it going now. I'm surprised we didn't hear each other. I didn't mean to frighten you."

He paused a moment to wipe his hands on a rag. He was never very good at guessing ages; he figured she must be in her fifties, but couldn't tell which end of that age range she leaned to. She was wrapped in a down-filled coat and wore those enormous Australian boots that were so popular. His wife lived in hers from October to May. She had a pair of glasses perched on her nose and was now regarding him imperiously through them.

"Welcome to Rosemont," he continued. "I understand you plan to put it on the market right away?"

Something about his polite, calm manner soon put her at ease. Judging by his weathered skin and full head of gray hair, she guessed he must be a few years her senior. She extended her hand to introduce herself and told him that she was most definitely not going to sell this place. Sam looked at her sharply and started to reply but stopped himself. Then, to her own astonishment, she announced, "As soon as my taxi returns, I'm going to check out of my hotel and move in here. Tonight. Permanently." She reached for the banister, as if to steady herself, and turned aside. *What are you doing?* she thought to herself. *You can't just up and move here. Are you nuts? What do you need with a six-bedroom house? Your family is in California, and so is your work.*

Maggie glanced back; Sam Torres was regarding her carefully. She wondered if he could sense that her decision to move into the house that night had been made impetuously on the spot.

"In that case," he said, "I'd better give you a complete tour. You'll need to know where all the entrances, switches, and thermostats are located." He gestured toward the library and began by showing her how to unlock and open the cantankerous old French doors. Sam nodded in the direction of the fireplace. "You won't want to start a fire until all of these chimneys have been cleaned and checked. This house hasn't been lived in for more than a decade." Sam paused and turned to Maggie. "Are you sure you want to move in here tonight? Once the plumbing is in use again, you'll find almost everything leaks. And the place hasn't been cleaned in years. Wouldn't you like to get it fixed up first?"

"No, I can live with all of that for a few days. As long as the furnace works and the electricity and water are turned on, I can cope."

"This sleet is supposed to turn to snow. You might get stranded up here," he cautioned as he produced a business card that read, "Sam the Handyman." "Here's my card. My cell phone number is on there. Why don't you call me when you get back tonight, and I can stop by to make sure that the furnace is still running and you're all set?" he offered.

"Thank you—very kind of you—but no need to drag out here later. I'll be fine," Maggie assured him with a confidence she didn't feel. For some reason, she felt completely comfortable with this concerned stranger. "Truthfully, this is a rash decision on my part."

Sam nodded.

"I can't explain it. I've never done anything like this in my entire life. But every fiber of my being tells me this is the right thing to do. For once in my adult life, I'm going to follow my intuition."

Sam regarded Maggie intently, and a slow smile lightened his worried expression. "In that case, moving in is exactly what you should do. Sounds like divine intuition. You should follow it. And you can always call me if anything comes up. My wife and I live about ten minutes away."

"Thank you, Sam. That makes me feel more comfortable." As they resumed their tour, Maggie was secretly relieved that Sam was making sure all the windows and doors were locked and all the thermostats were set. His instructions were thorough and helpful. It was evident that he knew the house well. The first floor had warmed to room temperature by the time they returned to the front door.

"I appreciate all you've done," Maggie said. "I'm not a dab hand at home repairs, so I'm sure I'll need your help on a regular basis. What do I owe you for today?" she asked as she turned toward her purse.

"Don't worry about that now," Sam said as he reached for the door. "We can settle up later. Would you like me to have the driveway plowed tomorrow?" She gratefully accepted. They said goodnight, and he headed out the door.

Later, in the eerie brightness of the nighttime snowstorm, Maggie and the taxi driver wrestled her suitcases and three bags of groceries to her front door. The driver helped her get them all inside and cautiously inquired if she would be okay there. She assured him she would be just fine, but she knew he doubted it, and, frankly, so did she. He had glanced at her in his rearview mirror occasionally on the drive out there and must have seen the waves of emotion surging through her. She went from feeling confident, intuitive, courageous, and spontaneous one moment to terrified, impulsive, incompetent, and irrational the next. She was known for her levelheaded, depend-able (and ultimately predictable) nature. Paul said he never wondered what she was thinking, and her kids swore they knew what she would say before she said it—and they were usually right. At times Maggie felt proud of this—she was understood, knowable, transparent. At other times, she felt dull and unimaginative. Well—this decision would surely make jaws drop.

As the taxi crept up the driveway toward her new life, fear and doubt were gaining the upper hand. She cleared her throat and was about to instruct the driver to take her back to the hotel when they again rounded the corner, and there it was. The house. *Her* house. Imposing, dependable, welcoming, strong. She would craft a happy future here.

She paid the driver, walked up the stone steps, and shut and locked the front door behind her. She toyed with the idea of phoning one of her children to let them know she changed her plans but decided against it. They could call her cell if they needed her. She wanted to savor her brave decision and her first night in her new home without the intrusion of their opinions.

Maggie picked up her groceries and headed in the direction of the kitchen. Dusty and in need of a thorough cleaning to be sure, but what a glorious kitchen! Beautiful walnut cabinets adorned with furniture-maker details soared to the twelve-foot ceiling. A huge window over the antique French sink and a smaller window over an old-fashioned copper vegetable sink would make the room irresistibly cheerful in daytime. The appliances and fixtures were outdated and would need to be replaced, but it was still the most beautiful kitchen she had ever seen—much less owned. *People will really have high expectations of a meal fixed here,* she mused. *I used to be such a good cook. I wonder if I can still muster up anything that does justice to this kitchen? I'll practice and get back on my game,* she decided with a bit of her characteristic determination.

Maggie stashed her groceries and dug into the rotisserie chicken and coleslaw that she bought for her dinner. She began a systematic reconnaissance of the kitchen. To her delight, it was equipped with every specialty pot, pan, and utensil imaginable. *I've been lusting after some of this stuff in catalogs for years,* she thought. *What great fun to cook in this kitchen.*

Along one wall was an enormous antique hutch. Maggie found it contained five complete sets of china, including specialty pieces like eggcups, double-handled soup bowls, and tureens. She recognized Colombia Enamel by Wedgwood and Botanic Garden by Portmeirion, but had to check the bottom of a plate to see that she had place settings for twelve of Derby Panel by Royal Crown Derby and a lovely blue-rimmed favorite called Autumn by Lenox. A set of cheerful yellow Fiestaware completed the collection. *Good Lord*—she felt faint. Maggie was a self-described china addict; now she had the collection to prove it. She vowed to use the good dishes every day.

Maggie made herself tea in a Wedgwood cup and wandered through the house to find a place to tuck herself away to enjoy it. The long day had taken its toll; she was exhausted. As she passed through the archway into the library, she found an overstuffed chair in the moonlight by the French doors and knew she had found her spot. Maggie dragged the sheet off the chair with one hand while waving away a cloud of dust with the other and settled into the chair's protective embrace.

An unblemished blanket of snow in the garden looked like frosting on a cake. At least four inches already, and it was still coming down hard. For the first time in months, everything around Maggie was quiet and still, and she felt peaceful. Thoughts of Paul were always crowding her, and they gradually settled on her now. Who was the man that she had been married to for over twenty-five years?

On the surface, Paul Martin was the charismatic president of Windsor College. Charming and handsome, with a killer smile. And laser focus. When he turned his attention on you, you felt like you were the most interesting and important person in the world. She had felt that way for years; had never doubted his integrity or fidelity. Mike and

Susan, now both grown and out of the nest, adored their father. Paul's unexpected death at the age of sixty-two had unearthed a number of betrayals. *Were there others yet undiscovered?* He evidently thought he had plenty of time to cover his tracks. Now Maggie was left to cope with it all.

The first shoe to drop was his embezzlement from the college. The interim president discovered suspicious receipts in Paul's desk, receipts that he had been careless enough to leave sitting in a drawer. An audit was hastily done and the results discreetly fed to her. Paul had been submitting fraudulent expenses as far back as they could trace, in excess of two million dollars. Where in the world had he been spending all of this money?

At first, Maggie wondered if Paul had a gambling problem. As she pored through the college's audit, however, it became very clear that the money was being spent in one location: Scottsdale, Arizona. And another fresh hell was born. She would never forget that day, last September, when she had summoned the courage to uncover the identity of the other woman.

Her short flight had been turbulent, and wedged into a middle seat between an overweight man with a dripping nose and a sprawling teenager; she was queasy by the time they landed. Taxiing to the gate seemed interminable. She snatched her carry-on from the seatback in front of her the moment they came to a stop, and shoved past the teen, jostling the woman in the seat across the aisle as she attempted to stand up. "Getting a bit claustrophobic in there," she muttered in a half-hearted apology. The woman huffed and fixed Maggie with an icy stare. She didn't care what anyone thought; she needed to get off of that damn plane. The line in front of her inched along to the door. Why in the hell were people so slow and clumsy with their luggage? Why did they insist on stuffing bags into the overhead bins that they couldn't handle on their own? *Just breathe deeply,* she told herself.

The rental car was waiting for her. Thank goodness for the perks of being a frequent traveler. She settled into the seat and turned the air conditioner on full blast. Maggie fumbled in her purse for the report the private investigator had given her. She double-checked the address, but didn't need to; it was seared into her heart. Maggie punched it into the GPS system, adjusted her mirrors, and began her journey.

It was only ten o'clock in the morning, but near-record temperatures were predicted and heat waves shimmered off the highway. The GPS was reliable, and she was close to the address in under thirty minutes. Maggie decided she needed something to drink and turned into a convenience store to get a giant diet cola and a bottle of cold water. No one was behind her in line, so she took her time fishing out the correct change. Now that she was here, she wasn't so sure she wanted to pick at this scab. She lingered over the rack of tabloid magazines by the door. What was the matter with her? She was just going to drive by a house. She probably wouldn't even see "her." She had come all of this way—she needed to hitch up her britches and do this thing.

Maggie coiled herself into the now oven-like car and burned her hands as she grasped the steering wheel. She took a long pull on her diet cola and set off once more. She drove slowly as the ascending street numbers indicated she was getting close. *Undeniably a swanky neighborhood,* she brooded. *Nicer than ours.* Spacious, new stucco homes with red-tile roofs and soaring arches. Intricate iron gates and ornate light fixtures. Manicured lawns tended by efficient landscapers. No signs of life on this oppressive day. Everyone was safely tucked away.

And there it was. Bigger than the rest—or was she imaging that? It was unquestionably the nicest house on the street. Bile rose in Maggie's throat. If you had lined up photos of all of the houses on that street and asked her which one Paul would have selected, Maggie knew it would have been this house. More grand than their home in California. Maggie drifted across the centerline and caught herself before she hit the other curb. Thank God she was the only car on the street. She needed to get hold of herself; she didn't want to get into an accident right outside the other woman's house. How cliché would that be? She was acting like a stalker, for goodness sake. No one could ever know she had done this.

She turned around in a driveway five houses down and drove past to view it from the other direction. It looked even better. *That bastard.* She tightened her grip on the steering wheel and turned the car around again, trying to find a shady spot along the curb where she could discreetly watch the house. A couple of palm trees provided the only shade available, and she pulled to the curb. The air conditioning was no match for the midday sun, and she felt like one of the ants that her brother would fry under a magnifying glass on the sidewalk when they were kids. Why in the world had Paul done this? Why hadn't they just divorced? Was he that concerned about the effect it would have on his career? Divorce wasn't a stigma anymore. And he evidently had plenty of money, so splitting what they had in California wouldn't have posed a problem. Surely he knew that she would never have gone digging for more. *Or was he addicted to the thrill of living a secret life?* She instinctively knew she had hit the mark dead center.

Her soda was long gone and she was taking the last swig of water, chiding herself that it was demeaning to be sweltering in a rental car outside of the other woman's house—then she appeared.

Maggie crouched over the dashboard, the air conditioning blasting her hair out of her face, and focused on the other woman like a laser. Tall, thin, and pretty—with shoulder-length blond hair and long, tanned legs—she was laughing with two school-aged children as she herded them into her Escalade. She pulled out of the driveway and glanced in Maggie's direction as she turned to say something to the children in the backseat.

Maggie clutched the steering wheel as nausea overwhelmed her. She tried unsuccessfully to choke it back and grabbed frantically for the empty soda cup and heaved violently. Sweating profusely, she fumbled in her purse for some tissues and a breath mint. The tears she had been holding back for months now broke free. This had been a stupid, crazy thing to do. Why had she expected it to turn out differently? She was a mess. Vomit on her cuff and in her hair. The last thing she wanted to do was spend the day here and get back on a plane later. To hell with the one-way drop-off charge for the rental car. It was only a six-hour drive. She'd be in her driveway about the same time as her scheduled flight was supposed to land. And she wouldn't have to see anyone or talk to anyone along the way. She swung the car around and set her course for home.

The minute she uncovered the Scottsdale connection, Maggie had a gut feeling about what she would find. Paul had supported a second family there. The investigator found that the two children weren't Paul's, thank God. But it had been a long-standing relationship and by the looks of the financial records, he had been supporting her handsomely. The most difficult part of Maggie's situation was bearing this knowledge alone; she dared not confide in anyone she knew.

Paul had been acting strangely after he took the post at Windsor College eight years ago. And Maggie had done her best to contrive an innocent explanation and rationalize Paul's odd behavior. But everything now made sense: the weekends away, when he was ostensibly too tied up in "strategic planning sessions" to call home; his trendy new wardrobe and haircut; and his younger, more "hip" vocabulary. When Susan pointed this out, Paul laughed and passed them off as his way of relating to the student body.

He had also become increasingly critical of Maggie's blossoming consulting business as a forensic accountant. At first, she believed he was genuinely concerned she was taking on too much and spreading herself too thin. He was emphatic that he needed her by his side for the numerous social engagements required by his position. Somewhere along the way she realized that he resented her success and her growing independence from him. Paul loved to tell his amusing little story about meeting the shy, studious, plain girl in college and turning her into the beautiful, polished, accomplished woman she was now; that their love story was a modern-day *My Fair Lady*. *Ugh!* She might not have been a sophisticate, but she hadn't been a country bumpkin, either. Even Eliza Doolittle outgrew the tutelage of Professor Higgins.

The turning point in their relationship was that horrible fight about the black-tie fundraiser he wanted to chair. He would turn up at the event in his tuxedo and make a nice podium speech, and she would work tirelessly on it for almost a year. She had begged him not to volunteer, told him that she simply didn't have the time, that just this once she needed to focus on herself first. She was about to land a lucrative expert witness engagement she had worked so hard to get. It was a fascinating case and would demand all of her time. And would undoubtedly lead to more such work. She simply could not turn it down.

Paul had railed that he couldn't turn the fundraiser down, either. He started on his usual refrain of "whose job pays more of the bills around here" when Maggie quietly pointed out that her income had exceeded his for several years. For the first time in their more than twenty years of marriage, Maggie had put her foot down and told Paul no. Paul had exploded and they had gone to bed angry. This time, however, Maggie didn't give in or apologize just to keep the peace.

They didn't speak for a week. When they tentatively resumed communication, Paul was derisive and demeaning, constantly criticizing Maggie in matters both large and small. But his opinion of her appearance, her job, and her social skills didn't matter much to her anymore. Maggie's friend Helen summed it up nicely: Paul had lost control of Maggie and he didn't like it. She had half-heartedly defended Paul, saying he was a leader and not a control freak, but she knew Helen was right.

Her lawyer negotiated a settlement of the college's claim against Paul's estate in exchange for his million-dollar life insurance policy. The board of regents hadn't been anxious to have their lax oversight of the college's finances exposed, and Maggie didn't want Mike and Susan hurt by a public discrediting of Paul's memory. She needed to get to the bottom of the mystery that was Paul Martin before she brought Mike and Susan into this nightmare. Maggie hired a private investigator that quickly uncovered the truth.

Revisiting these horribly hurtful revelations—so frustrating because Paul was not there to question, cross-examine, rage at—was like watching a tornado relentlessly obliterate her lovingly crafted life. The pain, loss, and desolation were constant companions. But tonight, sunk into this massive chair within the perfect stillness, Maggie removed herself from the starring role and felt like she was watching someone else's tragedy. She let her mind go blank and watched the snow slanting down across the trees outside her window. And she surrendered to a deep and dreamless sleep.

Having his office above his liquor store had its advantages; Chuck Delgado was well into the bottle of Jameson he grabbed from be-hind the counter as he waited for Frank Haynes to arrive on this Godforsaken night. Shortly after two in the morning, someone tapped quietly on the back door below. Delgado checked the security camera and buzzed him up.

Haynes firmly climbed the steps into Delgado's lair and found him slumped in his chair just outside the pool of light supplied by the green-shaded lamp on his desk. Haynes scanned the room, allowing his eyes to adjust to the dimness. The rest of the room was in shadow, and Haynes was glad of it. He didn't care to be accosted by Delgado's collection of crude, pornographic trinkets and toys.

Delgado shoved the open bottle and a highball glass in his direction. Haynes firmly declined. He didn't need to get lightheaded now, and God knows when that glass had last been washed. He cast a dubious glance at the two chairs across the desk from Delgado, and moved a stack of newspapers and a hamburger wrapper onto the floor. *At least he's eating at one of my restaurants,* he thought.

They regarded each other intently. Haynes remained silent.

Delgado nursed his drink and Haynes sat, brooding and impassive. Delgado finally sucked in a deep breath and began. "Okay, Frank, here's the thing. We ran into an unexpected situation."

Haynes raised an eyebrow.

"Not with anything here. Operations in Westbury are fine. In Florida. It's hard to keep your finger on things from a distance. I sent Wheeler down to check on things, but the bastard spent all his time with the whores in the condos. I understand a guy's gotta have fun, but he didn't do jack shit down there. Bastard lied to me when he got back. If this all goes down, he deserves to take the fall." Delgado gave a satisfied nod and sank back into his chair.

Haynes leaned rigidly forward, resting his elbows on his knees, and locked Delgado with his glare. He waited until Delgado, hand shaking, set his drink down.

"We aren't going to let this 'all go down,' Charles, now are we? We aren't going to let that happen. We had plenty of cushion built in to survive even the Recession. If you hadn't dipped your hand in the till, we wouldn't be having this unfortunate conversation."

"I had stuff to take care of. Those cops down there are expensive and—"

Haynes slammed a fist on the desk and roared, "Silence! I don't care what situation you got your sorry ass into. You know that you were not to bring your sordid business interests into our arrangement. Those condos were supposed to be legitimate investments, not whore houses or meth labs or whatever other Godforsaken activities you've got going in them."

Delgado held up a hand in a gesture of surrender. "You're right, Frank, I know you are. But stuff happens. I'll get this figured out. I may have buyers for a couple of the condos. And I'm expecting money from another associate next week. Enough to fund the shortfall in the next pension payments. Don't go gettin' yourself into an uproar. We'll get things straightened out. I'm on it," he slurred.

"You've got ten days to get this handled," Haynes growled. "I'm going to watch your every move from here on in. You won't want to disappoint me." His tone sent a wave of fear and dread through Delgado.

Haynes rose slowly, turned on his heel, and walked down the stairs, allowing the echo of his steps to recede before he opened the back door and was swallowed by the night.

Delgado held his breath until he could no longer hear Haynes' car retreating. "That guy is seriously unhinged." He reached for the bottle and didn't bother with a glass.

# Available at Amazon and for Kindle

Novels in the *Rosemont* series

*Coming to Rosemont*

*Weaving the Strands*

*Uncovering Secrets*

*Drawing Close*

Also by BARBARA HINSKE

**The Night Train**

*I'd love to hear from you!*

*Connect with me online:*

Visit **www.barbarahinske.com** to
sign up for my **newsletter** to receive your Free Gift,
plus Inside Scoops, Amazing Offers,
Bedtime Stories & Inspirations from Home.

**Facebook.com/BHinske**
**Twitter.com/BarbaraHinske**
Email me at **bhinske@gmail.com**

Search for **Barbara Hinske on YouTube**
for tours inside my own historic
home plus tips and tricks for busy women!

Find photos of fictional Rosemont, Westbury,
and things related to the Rosemont
series at **Pinterest.com/BarbaraHinske**

Made in the USA
San Bernardino, CA
18 September 2017